eighteen
plus

A graduate from the Shri Ram College of Commerce and an MBA from IIM Ahmedabad, Apurv Nagpal has worked in the corporate world in various capacities for over twenty years. His interests, other than writing, include sports (he has seen the last four FIFA Soccer World Cups live), travel (he has been to all the seven continents and once nearly drove to the North Pole), wines, cocktails and cinema (he regularly reviews the latest movies on his blog, www.apurvbollywood.blogspot.com.)

His Twitter handle is ApurvNagpal.

eighteen
plus

BEDTIME STORIES.
FOR GROWN-UPS.

APURV NAGPAL

RUPA

Published by
Rupa Publications India Pvt. Ltd 2013
7/16, Ansari Road, Daryaganj
New Delhi 110002

Sales centres:
Allahabad Bengaluru Chennai
Hyderabad Jaipur Kathmandu
Kolkata Mumbai

ISBN: 978-81-291-2982-6

First impression 2013

10 9 8 7 6 5 4 3 2 1

The moral right of the author has been asserted.

To

My sister Avani,
the angel of our family and our good luck charm.

My wife Ritu,
lots of love, thanks for the support,
and may you achieve what you dream of and fulfill
your true potential.

Contents

The Speaker Phone

'Sir, I'm really sorry to bother you on a Sunday, but you need to review and approve your press quote and the event flow.' Devyani's voice sounded urgent on the phone.

They were having a major function the next evening and the entire organization was running helter-skelter, either in office or glued to their laptops at home, getting things ready. He, Chandan Roy, the owner and CEO of his firm, was just about to have a relaxed Sunday brunch with his wife and some friends. 'I'll revert in an hour or so, if that's fine. And can you co-ordinate with Rishi for the brand side of things?' he said.

'Of course I will, sir, thanks, I'll call you back in an hour.'

He thought he heard a thud, but didn't think too much of it and put the phone down. Devyani handled corporate communications and, as usual, there were a few skirmishes happening with brand management. However, he was sure that she, a pert young thing who had been with the company for a couple of years, and Rishi, a brash, cocky young chap who handled brands, would be able to sort things out between them.

He heard his wife yell out to him again, complaining that he still hadn't sorted the mess in the kids' room, as he'd promised to, just as he remembered that he hadn't asked manufacturing to bring twenty extra samples of the product. Work or wife? As he called out to his wife that he would be there in a minute, he picked up the phone to call the head of manufacturing. He froze when he heard Devyani's voice. 'Stop it! I have to finish the presentation!'

She must've pressed the wrong button, he thought. Perhaps the speaker button instead of disconnect. He was just about to disconnect his phone when he heard Rishi's unmistakable voice. 'Fuck the presentation, babe! Fuck me!'

When Devyani giggled, he knew that he was on to a good thing. He walked into his study, put his phone on speaker mode and leaned back in his favourite armchair.

'Why do you women wear these skinny jeans? Don't you know they are so hard to remove?'

'Maybe it's a hint that I don't want anything removed?'

'You know, an Australian lawyer actually argued that his client couldn't have raped the woman, since the woman was wearing skinny jeans. That it was impossible to remove them without consent or help from the wearer. And the wise judge agreed!'

'So are you saying that I won't be able to press any rape charges if I'm wearing these?'

There was a pause before Rishi said, 'Any judge who has encountered these jeans will agree with me.'

There was a longer pause before Devyani replied, 'I'm undoing the top button and the ankle zips. But that's just because they're too tight. These actions in no way imply that I want the jeans removed or that I am aiding in their removal. Any judge will agree with me. Achcha, now go, let me finish this presentation.'

Chandan could hear keys being punched on the laptop. Then they stopped and were replaced by wet, smacking sounds which got progressively louder.

'Don't, Rishi!' A wet slurp. 'I seriously…' Lips smacking. '…have to…' A pause, with heavy breathing. '…work.' A long pause. 'Why don't you understand?'

'Understand? Yahaan meri jawani ke din udte jaa rahe hain and you want me to understand? Bewafa aurat, tumne mujhe ek maamuli presentation ke liye chhod diya?' Rishi's voice rang with mock anger.

Devyani giggled.

'Hai hai, yeh majboori, yeh mausam aur yeh doori,' Rishi began to sing. He's tuneless and out of breath. Chandan can't tell if he's just excited or dancing. 'Mujhe pal pal hai sataye, tere do takiyaan di naukri mein, mera lakhon ka saawan jaaye!'

The last word of the song was followed by the longest kiss so far, followed by several mini kisses. Chandan imagined he could hear the rustle of clothes being removed. Just as he heard faint moans and leaned forward, excited, his wife Ritika entered the room.

'Chandan…' she began, then froze when she recognized the sounds coming from his phone. 'Chandan, you pervert! Porn even in the daytime now!' she hissed as he hastily pressed the 'hold' button. 'We're having people over in a few minutes. Your friends. I'm going crazy trying to get everything ready and here you are, sitting in your study watching porn!'

She paused to catch her breath. Chandan's eyes involuntarily followed her ample breasts as they heaved dramatically. Catching his glance, Ritika said, 'You're sick, I tell you! You need help! Disgusting!' She slammed the door on her way out.

Chandan wanted to follow her but pressed the hold button for a quick check instead.

The moans had risen in volume. Chandan cast an agonized glance at the door, then at the phone, and decided to stay put.

'Rishi, no, don't. Not now.'

When her moans continued uninterrupted, he knew Rishi had decided to pay no heed.

'Rishi!'

'What?'

'Nothing!'

Then Chandan heard the sound of something being dragged, and then the keyboard tapping commenced. Devyani said, 'Let me work!'

Chandan fully commiserated with Rishi at the moment; he could imagine, all too well, the look of disappointment on his face.

The doorbell rang; it must be the first guests of the afternoon. After he heard Ritika bellow, 'Chandan Roy, open the door right now!' he rushed off, mentally thanking Devyani for being so dedicated to her work.

He was relieved to find Samrat and Simran, perhaps his most open-minded friends, at the door. He weighed the pros and cons in his mind and decided to go for it. In a few minutes they were all seated eagerly in his study and, when he pressed the hold button, he found that he had timed their arrival just right.

After a couple of minutes of heavy-duty moaning, Devyani said, 'Wait Rishi. The condoms!'

There was a deafening silence before Devyani's voice rose, shrill and annoyed, 'Rishi, how can you forget again! That's it. This is over.'

'But, babe…'

'Don't babe me! This is serious, Rishi, I can't take chances.'

'Look, I'm really sorry. Can't you take the i-pill or something?'

'I can't take contraceptives. They make me fat. And why should I stuff my body with hormones and chemicals just because you can't remember something as simple as carrying a condom!'

'I have an idea, just wait a sec. Don't put any clothes on.'

They could hear a door open and slam shut. Then Devyani sighed and the sounds of the keyboard resumed.

'That's so sweet,' Simran said, nudging Samrat. 'He's just like you. Do you think he is going to try a home-made condom like you did?'

Chandan's face lit up as Samrat rolled his eyes at his wife's indiscretion. 'What home-made condom?' Chandan asked, patting Samrat's knee.

Ritika walked into the study just as Simran, her back to the door, explained, 'Oho, it was nothing. He got some clingfilm from the kitchen and wrapped it around his dick.'

Seeing Samrat turn beetroot red as he looked over her shoulder, Simran turned around to see Ritika by the door, her mouth open. But it was Samrat who was the first to recover. He walked up to Ritika, saying brightly, 'How are you?' while holding his arms outstretched for a hug. But, on seeing her expression, he just patted her on the shoulder and returned to his seat. Simran, though, hugged Ritika, saying, 'Oye, you didn't tell me you had such a nice thing going. Hum jaldi aa jate.'

Chandan explained as succinctly as he could.

Ritika then turned to Chandan. 'So, is it over now? He doesn't have a condom.'

'No, no, this Rishi seems like an enterprising chap,' Samrat said. Hope lurked in his voice.

'Bilkul. If now we don't get any action bahut KLPD ho jayega,' Simran added. 'If this boy can't do something now, Chandan, you must fire him immediately for lack of enterprise!'

As Ritika poured out the drinks, Chandan hooked up his phone to his speaker system. As soon as everyone was settled, Rishi made his reappearance, as if on cue.

'Babe, got them!' he yelled.

Chandan, Samrat and Simran exchanged high-fives.

'How did you get them? From where?' Devyani asked.

'You remember the friend from college I met in the lift the last time I was here? I took a chance and went to his flat. Luckily, he had a few spare ones.'

'Noooo! Rishi Buddhiraja, I live here. I can't have my reputation ruined like this. How could you do this?'

But the sounds of slurping soon indicated that all had been forgiven.

In between her moans and Rishi's steady lapping, Devyani asked, 'What will he think of me?'

'Who?'

'Your friend!'

'Devyani, he will think how lucky I am to have you! Now stop making me speak.'

The doorbell rang again at the Roys's. The four quickly agreed that if the Singhs were at the door, they would continue, but if it was the Sharmas, they would have to stop. Luckily, it was the Singhs and in another few minutes, just as the action changed course, all six of them were in the study, glasses in hand.

By this time Rishi, who had been otherwise occupied so far, made himself heard. From his loud groans and grunts, it was clear that Devyani was applying herself with zeal and skill.

Chandan's mischievous streak surfaced and he called Rishi's phone. They could all hear Rishi's phone play 'Tu cheez badi hai mast mast'. This would provide all of them much cause for laughter later.

'Just leave it.'

'It's the boss, Devyani! That's the ringtone I have for him.'

The bed creaked as Rishi reached for the phone.

'Yes, sir!'

Chandan kept it brief. He was just checking to see that between Devyani and him, all issues had been sorted and everything was under control. On being reassured on both points, Chandan hung up.

'Yaar, bada dedicated ladka hai, I think he deserves a promotion. I wouldn't have taken the call,' Samrat said.

'As if I would have let you!' snorts Simran.

Devyani resumed her ministrations on Rishi with the earlier zeal, as demonstrated by his loud moans. Then the couple could hold off no longer and the bed began to violently creak and groan. Devyani and Rishi both climaxed together loudly. As the avid listeners basked in the couple's afterglow, Devyani sweetly asked Rishi to be a darling and get the strawberries and cream from the fridge.

Then, the Sharmas arrived.

■

At work on Monday, both Devyani and Rishi found a giant gift pack of strawberries and cream waiting for them at their desks. A very sweet note was attached to both: 'Just wanted to thank you for all the hard work yesterday—Chandan.'

■

Taking Care of a Hard-On

He woke up with a massive erection, a rare event at the age of forty, when even drinks in the evening can numb the senses—though they make everything more bearable and send one effortlessly to sleep.

He looked at his wife, his only option for sex at that moment. He was determined to not to let this particular hard-on go to waste, as had innumerable before, driven to limpness by his wife's prudishness and near-frigidity. He knew, though, that to get anywhere with her would take careful plotting. They had not been on talking terms since the last three nights thanks to some trivial issue, which he could no longer remember; but she would.

He debated his options in the bathroom. A full-frontal attack was out of the question. Others had been swiftly beaten off. As he walked out of the bathroom, she was changing, standing naked before the mirror, figuring out what to wear. The sight, as always, made him stop and stare. He knew from bitter experience that just walking up behind her and touching her on her lovely butt would only lead to a brisk tap on the offending hand and a disgusted, 'Is that all you think about?' Worse, it would effectively kill any chances of getting any sex for the next forty-eight hours.

She saw him looking at her, and raised her eyebrows in a silent 'why?' He went up to her and embraced her from behind, manoeuvring his body to conceal his erection. To his surprise, she didn't reject his touch nor did she bring up the fight. But he knew that the situation was delicate. Just one touch in the wrong place, just one mistimed caress or say, a playful tweaking of her nipples, would have the same impact as if he had suddenly been sprayed with skunk essence. So he took great care to control his impulses and kept his hands off all her erogenous zones. Then he made a near-fatal error. As a mood-setter, he decided to try a kiss, a gentle kiss. Not on the lips because that would mean getting right around her but a lingering peck on the cheek, ensuring that his lips were dry, just the way she liked it.

'Yuck, you smell horrible! Why haven't you brushed?' She disengaged swiftly and left him standing, in more ways than one.

By the time he finished cleaning his mouth, she was fully dressed, her choice of clothes a clear signal, if any were needed. They were nothing short of a chastity belt: a tight-fitting salwar-kameez that had multiple buttons on either side. From previous attempts he remembered that it needed to be literally peeled off her; the process never took less than forty-five minutes. Thinking fast, he went to the bed and switched on the TV. If he could find something interesting on any of the channels, she might sit down beside him, giving him a fresh window of opportunity. These were the moments when he missed being abroad, where nudity on TV is not really a problem.

Flicking the channels desperately, trying to find something appropriate, he knew that he was racing against time. If she left the room, there was no telling when she would return, as she would plunge into the world of cleaning and cooking. In the first positive development of the day, he saw a rerun of *Two and a Half Men* coming up, a reasonably raunchy episode, too. He knew that she liked the series and sure enough, drawn like a moth to a flame, she sat down on the bed, not too far from him. He felt a twinge of sadness at what life had reduced them to; even if he did a nude version of the Dance of the Seven Veils, she wouldn't have given it a second glance and would have walked out, but *Two and a Half Men*? No, that was a surefire showstopper.

No negative thoughts, no negative thoughts, he mentally berated himself and focused on the next steps. That salwar-kameez didn't leave much scope for manoeuvre. To get her to undress without ripping off her clothes was his next objective. He sidled up and sat next to her and then decided to go for broke: he swung his leg carelessly, casually, over her thigh, and reached for her hand. She swatted him away.

'The maid will be coming with tea,' she said, disengaging and moving a foot away. From bitter experience he knew that protestations about them being legally married, being therefore entitled to sit in close proximity wouldn't work. The maid was more precious than he was. After all, it had taken his wife longer to find the maid than it had taken her to find him. Nothing might ever be done which had the slightest possibility of upsetting her.

He decided to try the health route. 'Those mosquito bites on your leg? Show me? How are they healing?' he asked in his most solicitous voice.

'I can't lift up my salwar,' she said, without taking her eyes off Charlie Sheen. And then she twisted the knife in further. 'Teen din se to khayal nahin aaya mosquito bites ka?'

This time she did look at him for a millisecond, but he was grateful it wasn't for longer as it was a ice-cold glance of high intensity.

He had a diagonal rear-side view of her as she sat and watched the TV. It was a view that pleased him and his hard-on. He felt a lot of pride in this particular hard-on which, despite all the negativity thrown at it, had managed to keep the flag flying. It only renewed his desire to make sure it got what it deserved. He decided to recharge briefly and began to take deliberate and imaginative note of her contours. The salwar-kameez was tight enough to leave nothing much to the imagination. Breasts, first. Once again, as often before, he bemoaned her choice of bra. It could defeat Superman's X-Ray vision. So thick was it. But then, his persistence paid off. He realized that if you looked hard enough, you could make out where it ended and where the swell of her breast began. Her breasts began to jiggle. A good sign. She was laughing. He joined in, too, just to show that he had been watching the TV as well. He also realized that he did not need to feed his hard-on; he was raring to go. He needed to find a way to get his hands on her breasts. The episode would end in ten minutes. Luckily, the maid came in just then, set down Madam's tea and left.

He promptly moved in again and wrapped his legs around her. The twinge in his knees reminded him that he needed to begin yoga again, but keeping the 'mard ko dard nahin' motto in mind, he focused on the task at hand.

He gently kissed the nape of her neck while running his hand down her back. Five minutes to go. He had to get her in the mood in the next five minutes or household chores would triumph over his manhood. And he had to do it by stealth, not disturbing her TV viewing till the serial ended. He restructured the problem in his head as if it were an algorithm. He had to have her sufficiently in the mood to keep sitting down when the serial ended but without disturbing her current viewing pleasure. If he got the balance right, he would have another couple of minutes, once it had ended, for her to decide whether to let him proceed or not. Until then: Slowlee. Slowlee. Catchee. Monkee.

He renewed his efforts, rubbing her back in long, slow suggestive strokes, staying deliberately clear of both her erogenous and tickle zones. It was almost as if it there was a narrow path etched out on her back, with several no-entry and one-way signs around it. One false move, one departure from the straight and the narrow would lead to an instant rejection. A career defusing landmines could have been his, he mused. However, such thoughts didn't help his erection so he shook his head vigorously, keeping his focus on her back. Firm on the back, delicate on the neck. Firm on the back, delicate on the neck…

From the way her body relaxed, he could tell he was succeeding. The end credits began to roll and he widened his path to include the breasts, cupping them firmly from below, then releasing them and brushing her nipples gently with his fingers. The stinging tap on his wrist told him that he had moved too fast. He had forgotten the joke that comes after the credits. He patiently returned to his old routine, 'firm on the back, delicate on the neck', till the show ended. He then moved to the front, rubbing her inner thighs and working his way up to her breasts and then back again, again remembering where to be firm and where to keep his touch light. It was working. It had been a full two minutes since the show had ended and she was still sitting there, not talking to him but looking blankly at the TV. He decided it was time to move to phase two of his plan.

This time, when his hands reached her breasts, only one returned southwards. The other gently moved up and then froze when it encountered the maze of threads which barricaded her neckline. It was tied in a couple of knots with two strings hanging loose. Pull the right one and it would all open up, as if by magic. Tug at the wrong one and her neckline would tighten and the moment would be lost forever. He knew her low tolerance for pain and also knew that he would have to spend the next fifteen minutes just repairing the damage. God was on his side, though, and even though his eyes closed with trepidation as he tugged, it was the right string. He could also make out from the quickening of her breathing that he had timed it right. However, it was critical that he didn't speed up too much. He could recall many a bitter moment when he had lost the battle at this crucial juncture. He now graduated from kissing her neck to also kissing her earlobe. This, again, was a move not without risk. Until a couple of years ago, the earlobe had been a surefire arouser. Of late, though, it had again become one of those get it right and it was 'hallelujah!' but one wrong move and it was all over. The kiss had to be on the edge of the ear, not on the ear itself. Teasing with the finger didn't work, it had to be the lips but they MUST NEVER be wet (a sure turn-off). A little breathing inside the ear was fine but if he got the volume of air wrong, it could either result in her turning his face away from hers or worse, it might tickle her and that would be that. He focused determinedly on the back of the ear, a part where there was a fifty per cent probability of arousal but at least none of rejection. A couple of minutes later, he slipped his fingers through the threads guarding her neckline and towards her encased-in-padded-armour breasts. He didn't have much room to play with, given the tightness of her kameez, but gently eased his fingers underneath the padding, cupped her breast and waited for the inevitable query. And sure enough, ten seconds later, it came. 'What are you doing?' she whispered.

He had never been able to get over this. Was it a rhetorical question? He had tried ignoring it in the past but then had seen it being repeated. Was it a trick question? Was it one that had no right answer? As always, he fought down the impulse to reply with any of the fifty snappy retorts bubbling up in his brain and decided to maintain a steady silence, punctuated only by heavy breathing. This was not the time for humour. Encouraged by the fact that her voice had now dropped to a whisper, instead of her normal shrill, high-treble tone, he waded in deeper, rising up behind her and now putting both hands inside the neckline, cupping both breasts, hands moving in circles, stretching the fabric of her kameez fully. After a while, he removed one hand and, swiftly opening the cord of the salwar around her waist with it, slid it inside. As always, he loved the soft feel of her pubic hair and the warmth. A few seconds later she leaned her body back against his and it was at that moment that he knew she was his. Two minutes later he had her bottom off, and five minutes later, with considerable help from her, he had her top off. Opening bras was one of his specialties. Normally he liked to challenge himself, using only one hand; only if that didn't work would he move to using both. Given the criticality of the situation, though, and all that had preceded it, he decided to play it safe this time. Preferring precision over passion, he used both hands and succeeded on his first attempt.

They were both naked now, he on top of her, about to enter. She looked at him with wide, mournful eyes, 'What happened that night? Why did you yell at me?'

He'd never been able to get his head around this fundamental difference between how men and women were wired. For him, such issues could be easily discussed and amicable solutions reached during post-coital intimacy. He'd always felt that if more world leaders had sex, the globe would be a happier place and beset with lessen problems. There were very few things which couldn't be agreed upon in the afterglow, when everything was viewed through rose-tinted glasses, the birds seemed to be chirping and the sun was at its cheerful best. He decided silence was the best defense again and kissed her on the lips to ensure that it applied both ways.

■

Fifteen minutes later, the deed was done, both were comfortable, both were naked and in each other's arms, awash in the soft afterglow of mutual orgasms.

'How was it for you?' he asked tenderly.

'Very good,' she replied with a smile, 'I was really in the mood. I have been having "nice" dreams all week.'

He smiled ruefully as he reached for the both of his favourite tipple, kept at his bedside. Women, he thought, the reason why I drink so much nowadays.

Going Down to Rise Up

'Ladies, I now want you all to welcome our keynote speaker. She is going to talk about something important, something that affects, or has the potential to affect, our lives on a day to day basis. Blowjobs. So, a round of warm applause for Meena Verma.'

This welcome address was being given at the Ladies' Kitty Party Group's North Zone conference being held in Delhi at one of the posh five star hotels of Delhi. It was under the aegis of Preeti Sharma, their dynamic, roly-poly president, that they had decided to devote an entire half-day to talking about sex. And in the most controversial move yet, which had brought the crowd of one hundred placard-waving, protesting women outside the venue as the group inside put their hands together for Meena Verma, they had decided to have a talk on blowjobs. Attendance for this speech was the highest amongst all the talks which had been held so far.

Meena climbed the stage slowly. She was dressed in a stylish salwar kameez, and an embroidered dupatta was slung over one shoulder in such a way that it did not obstruct the view of the diamond necklace which nestled between her ample breasts. The necklace was rumoured to be worth at least sixty lakhs.

Mrs Gupta, who was busy eating chicken lollipops, looked around her table and asked, 'Do you know how Meena got famous for blowjobs?' Pausing for a pregnant moment, she answered her own question, 'Word of mouth!' before dissolving into peals of laughter. Half the women at her the table didn't get the joke.

Meena quickly checked that her laptop was connected to the projector, and confirmed with the technician how to scroll down her presentation slide. Though a sharp cookie, well-travelled, intelligent and articulate, Meena's lack of computer skills, despite being vice president in a computer firm, was almost as legendary as her dexterity at blowjobs. She nodded, cleared her throat, checked her mike and began.

'My friends, I have a mouth which makes men think of blowjobs. But I didn't know that for the first ten years of my sexually-active life. I did occasionally wonder, in that period, why all my men had always been so keen on oral sex, but had never really got to the bottom of the matter. Though, to be fair, my kitty party group did try to tell me indirectly. But I didn't heed their hints.'

Mrs Aggarwal on Table 15 and Mrs Khemani on Table 3 nod vigorously and look around their tables for acknowledgement as Meena continues.

'They asked me to apply my lipstick differently, to not accentuate the curve of my lips. And they virtually begged me to change my shade of lipstick, a bright red that screamed for attention when darker, less obtrusive shades could probably have helped. But,' Meena smacks her ruby red lips and carries on,

'I was adamant back then about bright red, my favourite colour since childhood, and I am still partial to it.'

Miss Reema on Table 4 leans forward and whispers conspiratorially to her companions, 'We gifted her so many lipsticks in darker shades, but she never used them.'

Meena picks up a glass of water, takes a quick sip, and places the glass back on the table. The smudge of red on the rim of the glass is visible even from the back of the room. 'I also had a vast array of dresses and lingerie in the same shade as well, so changing colours was really out of the question, given my relative poverty during those days.' She emphasizes the point with a hand movement also designed to show off the solid rock gracing her finger. Her days of penury are definitely a thing of the past.

'Does anyone here know who invented the lipstick and why?' She glances around quickly and when no guesses are forthcoming, answers, 'It was the Egyptians, who wanted to distinguish the oral-sex workers from the others.'

Many women go 'ooh' and 'aah', while a couple nod knowledgeably, pretending that they knew the answer but didn't speak up. Intrigued by the general reaction, Mrs Lal, Table 19, whose English isn't very good, nudges Mrs Saxena, 'Ki boli, kudi?'

Mrs Saxena begins helpfully, 'Oh das rahi sigi ki lipstick di shuruaat Egypt wich hoi si. Uthe wo...' She frowns, trying to frame the words 'wo...' and then gives up. 'Chaddo, main tvanu baad wich dasangi,' she says and downs her Bloody Mary in a single gulp.

Meena begins again, dramatically, 'I still remember. Even the first time I got naked with a man, when I had thought I was going to make love for the first time, even then he had been keener on a blowjob than on sex. He had guided me down there first and then, when I resisted, almost forced my head down. Most men over the next few years were like him, leading to a kind of a Vicious Cycle.' Her first slide now comes on.

THE VICIOUS CYCLE

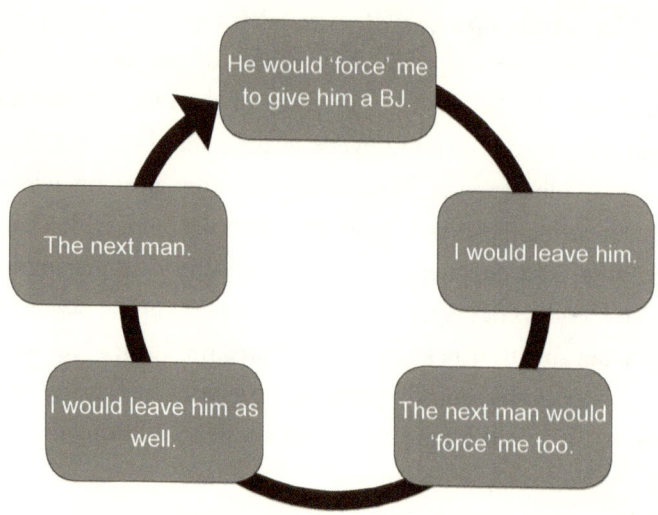

He would 'force' me to give him a BJ.

I would leave him.

The next man would 'force' me too.

I would leave him as well.

The next man.

'Every man I met would try to force me to give him a blowjob. I would leave him and find a new man. He would also try to force me to suck, so on and so forth. And the net result was that I began to hate blowjobs and I stopped giving them. I began to date fewer and fewer men, stopped enjoying sex and was even in depression for a few years.'

'Until,' she pauses dramatically, 'I had a life-changing chat with a doctor friend of mine who pointed out to me the possibilities the shape of my mouth and the curve of my lips presented. He said my natural pout simply screamed BLOWJOBS to every red-blooded male on the planet. He advised me to twist it to my advantage. He taught me a profound truth, one which has changed my life, and one which will change yours!'

Her next slide is fairly self-explanatory but she yells each point out loud, saying the words slowly, and some of the women in the audience begin to nod. A couple of women even make notes on the pad in front of them.

THE UNIVERSAL INSTRUCTIONS

1. Use blowjobs as a bargaining chip.

2. Use blowjobs to get your way.

3. Use blowjobs to get ahead.

She then says, 'Let me illustrate my point now with some key data I have collected over the last eight years, after my life-changing moment.'

THE AVERAGE GIFT VALUE EXPRESSED IN RUPEES/GIFT

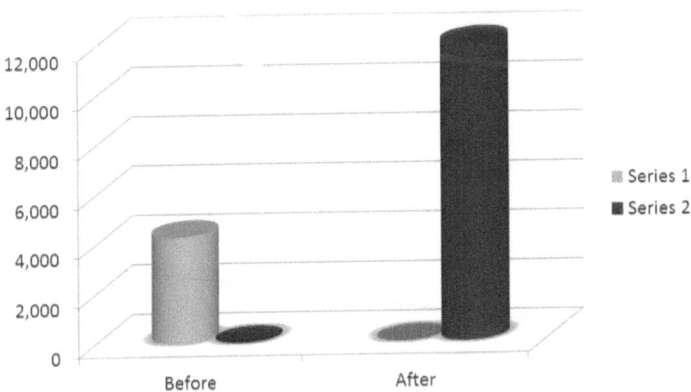

'As you can see, the average value of gifts I receive from my men has gone up dramatically, by almost three times. And, in fact, as I've got better at what I do, the gift value has gone up even more.'

THE LAST THREE YEARS VS THE INITIAL YEARS

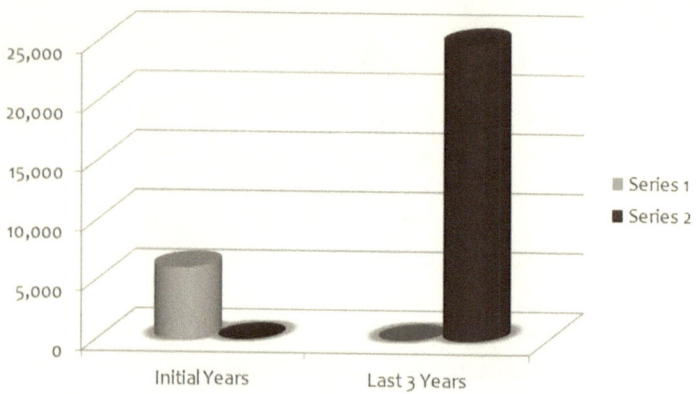

Some women in the audience gasp and the women who are taking notes scribble numbers furiously. Mrs Sejal, a slim chartered accountant with a rather stern disposition, says aloud to no one in particular, 'Her last three years' average is almost three times her "before" average,' and nods, impressed.

Meena's next slide, the showstopper, is greeted by tumultuous applause.

PROMOTIONS

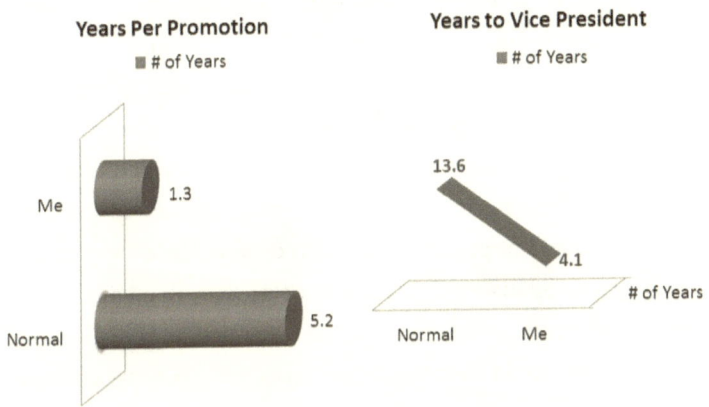

Years Per Promotion

▪ # of Years

Me — 1.3

Normal — 5.2

Years to Vice President

▪ # of Years

13.6

4.1

# of Years

Normal   Me

'How many career women can boast statistics like this?' Meena asks triumphantly. 'And I can assure you, friends, that I have earned my promotions as much as any other person in the organization. I am the youngest VP in my company's history. Ever!' A standing ovation follows until Meena motions everyone to sit down again.

'Another upside is, my colleagues and bosses very rarely disagree with anything I say or do. Do you know that I have been on thirty-two foreign trips in the four years that I have been in this company? None of my fellow VPs have been on more than five?' Applause is about to begin again, but is quickly hushed by Meena.

'Now that I've explained the advantages of blowjobs, I want you all to understand why they work. 'They work because men are lazy, selfish bastards who can rarely look beyond their own pleasure. They work because men are weak creatures. They work because there are a very few women who willingly pleasure them this way. They work because just before a man receives a promised blowjob, there is little to which he will not agree.' Excited murmurs and small conversations break out all over the room.

Meena raises her volume. 'I'm not saying this to run men down. And I do not say it with any any degree of vindictiveness. I'm just telling you about things as they are so that you understand the nature of the beast you're dealing with and how to use it to your advantage. I hope the implications of what I said are perfectly clear. Always negotiate before the gift, never after. Remember, your target is inherently selfish and, after he is satisfied, may not agree to as much as he would have just before. Also, while making promises after the event, he is balancing what he has to give with the likely estimation of future favours expected. You don't want to be in that situation. Just before the blowjob, he is completely unable to think of anything beyond the imminent treat that awaits him.'

Mrs Sejal, the slim chartered accountant has her palm on her forehead. She exclaims, 'So that was what I was doing wrong!'

Meena looks at her and nods knowingly. 'I now want to turn your attention to the best way to give pleasure. I've ignored the obvious stuff, just kind of summarized a few special "how-tos" on blowjobs based on my considerable experience. Tip one, pun intended, is to always focus on the tip.' Her next slide shows a biological diagram of a penis in all its glory.

Meena ignores the crowd's reaction and instead uses her laser pointer to highlight the anatomical part she is referring to. 'Note the high concentration of blood corpuscles on the tip versus the other parts. That's where he is the most sensitive, the most vulnerable. My recommendation is to use the tongue here for maximum impact.

'Next point, never go down if you've just eaten something. You might be nauseous. My personal rule is to always wait twenty minutes if I've eaten something and at least five minutes if I have had something to drink.

'Next, always use your hands. Don't just let them dangle uselessly but bring them into active play. Gently rub his balls or his thighs or his chest. Remember, a blowjob is forty-two per cent quicker if hands are used.

'Third and last, foreplay is as important for them as it is for us, when we're having sex. If you spend just a few moments stroking him, kissing him, you can make him come thirty-six per cent quicker than if you get down to it immediately. So this is what I call the Multiplier Effect. If you indulge in some foreplay and use your hands, you could be done almost seventy-five per cent quicker than if you did neither. And each moment here is a moment less with his dick in your mouth. That's all I have to say. I now throw the floor open for questions, I've been told we have time for three questions.'

Mrs Kazmi, all of fifty-two years old, surprises everyone by asking the first question. 'Beti, do circumcised penises have less sensitivity at the tip than normal ones do?'

Meena knows exactly where she is coming from. 'That's a very good question, Aunty. Contrary to popular belief, scientific studies and my own personal observations have shown there is no difference between the two.'

Mrs Kaushik, who teaches Hindi in a school, is the next surprise candidate. 'Par, beta,' she asks with a grimace. 'Yeh aadmi log itne gande hote hain, kabhi uchit tarah se saaf to karte nahin hain. Is vishay par koi sujhav aapka?' She sits down to general approval from the gathering. She has obviously touched a raw nerve.

Meena has been expecting this question. 'Remember the first thing I said about men: they are selfish, lazy bastards! You have to clean them up. You cannot expect that they will do anything to achieve our high standards of cleanliness. The solution is very simple...' She fishes out a packet of baby wipes from her handbag. 'I never leave home without these now and I never begin anything until I have thoroughly wiped it clean to my satisfaction. You have to wait for about fifteen seconds for the alcohol to dry off. Another advantage is that they are also perfumed.' She lifts her pack up so that everyone can see. 'I prefer this particular brand because it contains aloe vera and a nice, subtle fragrance, which is not overpowering.'

Mrs Kaushik takes a good hard look at the brand and notes its name down on her cellphone, and starts thoughtfully nodding to herself.

Mrs Titus, newly married, stands up to ask the next question. 'Miss Meena,' she begins confidently, but then pauses to blush furiously. 'What is your point of view on...' she pauses again, her face a bright red, 'on...on...swallowing?' There is a sharp intake of breath all around. This question has clearly been on everyone's minds.

Mrs Lal, Table 19, nudges Mrs Saxena again, 'Ae ki poochiya kudi ne?' but Mrs Saxena raises her hand for silence, concentrating intensely on the answer.

Meena smiles. 'Wow, great question, and one of the frequent dilemmas we women face. My advice here is to go with what you're comfortable with and not push yourself or be forced into doing it. Men do go a little weaker in the knees if you swallow than if you don't. So there is an advantage if you do it. And my advice, if you do decide to do it, is to not begin doing this right from the beginning but only later in a relationship. Make it a special treat for your guy.' With that, she moves away from the podium to a standing ovation that lasts for seventeen minutes.

■

Meena was later invited to speak at the Ladies' Kitty Party Group's West, East and South Zone conferences. The last was the the only group in which there were some hecklers. A particularly prudish lot even staged a walkout midway through her talk.

Shortly later, Meena was given a promotion and appointed general manager, thanks to her boss' effusive praise. She is, till today, the youngest ever employee in the company to become country head.

■

Eighteen Things that Arouse

1. When you kiss her, the lingering taste of cigarette smoke on her breath.
2. The curve of her breast as it sweeps sharply upward and meets the nipple at its peak.
3. The smell of her smooth underarms.
4. The lovely, soft curls of untrimmed pubic hair.
5. The warmth of her loins. When her mere presence next to you sends the mercury up by a few degrees.
6. The precise point where the rounded arc of her splendid buttock ends, and the small arc of the back of her thigh begins.
7. Every woman singer with a husky voice. Suzanne Vega. Norah Jones. Dido. Sade.
8. Playing with her nipples until they are erect.
9. Feeling her hot breath in your ear.
10. Making her come. That moment when she arches her back, eyes closed, her hands tightly clenching your shoulders, then

the shudder which runs through her entire body. Afterwards, the tenderness in her eyes as she gazes at you.

11. Spicy stories about sex. The more spontaneous, the more unprompted, the better.

12. Spreading apart her two cheeks and placing your finger there. The feeling of having her flesh close in on your finger.

13. When she kisses your nipples lightly, teasing each in turn.

14. Bathing her. Lukewarm water, lavender-and-patchouli-scented soap, some suds and a hand shower.

15. Cuddling together naked, your limbs intertwined

16. That time between the third and the fifth drink. When she is high enough to drop her inhibitions but not high enough to fall asleep.

17. Running the tips of your fingers on her naked skin, watching her twitch and turn.

18. Watching her undress. Every time.

■

The Corner Room

'Could you please book a room in a corner or far away from the others? I am very loud.' She giggled.

This was their first phone conversation, one they were having after hours of intense texting.

■

It had begun innocently, a couple of work-related texts from her, and his replies which were equally straightforward. It was hard to pinpoint now what had led them here, six years after their first meeting. She was with a media agency, he in a blue-chip multinational. They had met several times, even with respective spouses, and no hint of anything other than work had passed between them. And then, one day, while they were in different cities, the penny had dropped.

It had been his first time sexting and he had been surprised by how easily it worked. She didn't need flourishes or flowers. Even direct messages like 'I love your boobs' had brought a drizzle of emoticons in reply. Her messages ('I want to feel you inside me, now!' and 'How many times do you think you can do it in one night? I can go all night!') had made him miss many slides in dull conferences. He could sense his colleagues' bewilderment, and wondered if any of them guessed, especially when he caught himself smiling. But then he had decided not to care.

■

Because the nth intimate detail had been exchanged between them through texts, he wondered what they could talk about when they met. Talk was not really on her agenda. She arrived by the evening flight, he skipped the conference dinner, they met at his hotel, the bottle of wine proved unnecessary and they got down to business the moment she stepped through the door of his hotel room.

She hadn't been lying about the moans. He had never encountered anything quite like it. It didn't take much to get them to start either. They began while he was still undressing her and got louder in intensity as he moved his hands over her, reaching ear-busting levels by the time they actually began fucking. She was much younger than him, curvaceous, with a firm figure and a delectable rack. He enjoyed making sure neither of her breasts felt neglected. She couldn't wriggle out of her panties fast enough. Even before he had unbuckled his belt, she had his zip down and was caressing him using both hands alternately—an interesting variation which he had never encountered before. He had promised to kiss every square inch of her and he began to make good on his promise, rolling her over on her stomach and sitting on top of her, just below her buttocks. He began with her back, working all over with a combination of lips, tongue and fingers, her increasing groans spurring him on. Everyone, he realized, loves an audience, loves to be appreciated. He had never encountered anyone so responsive to his every move and that made him increasingly bolder.

Then he turned his attention to her pert ass. As he widened her buttocks with his fingers, he thought of the text in which she had said that she loved anal attention. That text had aroused him more than any other. After some careful oral attention to that particular part of her anatomy, his ears thankfully cushioned by her buttocks, he inched down her legs and all the way to the soles of her feet. When he finished with her toes, he flipped her over and, holding one leg up, he slid down her inner leg with his tongue, all the way to her pussy. She did not keep her pubic hair, a ritual she had followed strictly from the time she was a teenager. By the time he reached the end of the road with the second leg, she was in no mood to let him continue with the kisses and eased him inside her.

The disadvantage of the frenzied moaning was that since it was already at fever pitch, there was no way of sensing if she had already come, was coming or going to come. Blindsided, he kept going at a frenetic pace till his own ejaculation finally made him slow down. She grabbed a buttock, squeezing it hard, wrapping her legs tightly around him as he came inside her. (She had taken a pill so they could bareback.) He, in turn, hadn't come inside anyone for a really long time and that enhanced his pleasure as well. Shudders ran up and down his body as she tried to wring every last drop of cum from him.

He rolled over, body spent, bathed in sweat a took a few deep breaths. He felt that he deserved a Nobel Prize for Humping. If he had been a smoker, he would've lit a Cohiba. Heck, given their recently concluded epic session, even the neighbours might have lit some admiring cigarettes.

Her Turn

But she wasn't done. She hadn't been kidding about going on all night. She brought a towel soaked in cold water and began to sponge him, blowing softly over the areas she rubbed down, cooling him and then warming him up again. She did his nipples first, lavishing great care on each, circling them, prodding them, blowing over them, teasing them with her tongue and ending with a naughty little bite. His nipples had never received such individual attention before. She then moved to his underarms, then down to his stomach, his legs and followed them down to his toes.

Finally, she turned her full attention on his dick. She rubbed it first with a wet towel and followed that up with one soaked in hot water. Then again. And again. It was still limp when she took it inside her mouth and ran her tongue over every centimetre, rolling her tongue around the tip for a long time. She let it out and also immediately bathed it in a warm rivulet of saliva. She ignored his feeble protestations and repeated the cycle: hot water, cold water, inside the mouth—a thorough working over. By this time, his penis had begun to respond and reached a semi-erect state and she paused to admire her handiwork, and then redoubled her efforts.

Now her tongue and lips took only the tip inside, leaving the rest of the penis out in the cold. Within a few minutes, he had achieved a full erection. Her tongue stroked his entire penis, from base to tip, from all rides. And finally, just as it began to throb, she took it inside and made him come, using her hands to skillfully stroke his thighs. He had only seen women swallow in porn movies. This was a notable first, and gave him shudders of the kind he had never experienced before.

The bottle of wine now came in handy. They both sat back, switched on the TV, and began watching the latest Bollywood music videos, kissing and sipping, kissing and sipping. They ran a scientific experiment to see if the wine, if passed from her mouth to his, tasted sweeter than from his mouth to hers, but results proved inconclusive.

It felt as if they had known each other for years, as if they could say anything, think anything. The sex had connected them and had dissolved the inhibitions they normally felt. She tried to sing along one of the newer numbers, confessing that she normally never sang outside the confines of her shower cubicle. He showed off with his voice a bit, crooning one of the more soulful songs and impressing her by being able to explain some of the Urdu. About an hour later, the wine bottle empty, they were both belting out old Hindi film numbers, all cares shoved aside. Then it was time for a quick shower.

The bathtub was a welcome luxury. They sat on the edge

of the tub, naked, watching the water fill, chatting about this and that. He asked housekeeping for bubble bath, blasé about doing so even at that late hour, and the entire room soon smelt of lavender; mountains of foam covered the entire bathtub. They slipped into the tub on opposite sides. He gallantly took the one with the taps and gave her the one with the headrest. They soaked in the warmth for the first few minutes, their heads back, their bodies lying easily next to each other, the foam all around them softening the water and making it seem more welcoming.

Her feet made the first move, quickly seeking out his crotch. His protests of 'It's only been half an hour' were brushed aside, in this case almost literally. Deciding offense was the best defence, his feet moved into action as well, but her moans quickly dispelled any thoughts of a quiet, restful soak. She now used her hands to guide his foot and, her head thrown back, used her foot to play footsie with his tired penis. Was it the warm water? Was it the rejuvenating qualities of lavender? The foam? Her expert ministrations? Whatever, it was, it wasn't long before they were at it again. She was on top of him, her legs wrapped around his back as he half sat, half slouched against the side of the bathtub. Water splashed and gurgled, their rocking motion unleashing a miniature tsunami inside the tub and creating a miniature Lake District on the bathroom floor. Some of the waves could also have been be cause of the sheer sound energy of her moans. In the confines of the bathroom, they acquired a unique acoustic echo. She came multiple times, her orgasms not only audible but also visible as her arms thrashed in the water. He came again and her knowing smile let him know that she felt his pulsations—and his surprise.

They used the towels to first dry themselves up and then spread them on the bathroom floor in a feeble attempt to clean up. The housekeeping staff was sure to find enough material to gossip anyway so they gave up after a while and drifted off into a peaceful sleep.

In a couple of hours, his eyes opened thanks to her hand massaging his nether regions. They made love twice again before going down for breakfast. She ordered a yogurt and an egg-whites-only omelette. He felt he could splurge on a paneer paratha with the works.

He caught her eyeing his paratha and fed her small bites, dabbed with a little bit of mango achaar and spoons of dahi as accompaniment. They both left a little later, heading their separate ways in their separate cars.

■

Years later, they met in another city, at another hotel, and caught up for a few minutes at the coffee shop. Memories of the night came flooding back for both. He remembered the surprise he had felt on his fifth orgasm, the tiny dribble of it, but what a magnificent achievement it had been.

What she remembered most of all was that he had lovingly fed her his paratha.

■

La Senza

He had a couple of hours to kill between his meetings at the mall. Not long enough to watch a movie—though he was tempted to go in for something he had already seen and just walk out when time ran out. The list of available films settled it. It was a week of mindless comedies, it seemed, in both English and Hindi, the former a teen road movie and the latter something starring Tusshar Kapoor.

He decided to walk around instead. It was afternoon, a weekday, the crowd sparse, just the way he liked it. He wasn't hungry and for the last few years he had been watching how much he ate, rather than the usual 'what he ate'. He was slimmer than ever as a result, and relatives and friends alike cast envious glances at his lean torso. Mentally striking off butter chicken and naan, he decided to do some window-shopping.

It was in the Western-dress section of Shoppers Stop that he first noticed her giving him the once over. He was admiring the cut of a strapless dress draped over a mannequin, while she, dressed in a yellow, floral, knee-length, summery dress was looking at something a bit more formal: a black, full-length dress with an inviting cleavage.

'Excuse me, sir,' a shop assistant at his elbow spoke tentatively, 'but we don't have this dress in large size.'

'But, I never…'

'Sorry,' Yellow Dress walked up. 'I believe that's mine,' she said, smiling at the shop assistant.

The shop assistant apologized and left.

'Medium should be fine for you, no,' he said, with his best smile.

She smiled too. 'I wish,' she said, and left to examine the black dress again. As he went to the men's section, he thought, That's that. Fifteen minutes later, he was looking at some costume jewellery when she walked into the shop.

'Oh, hi,' she said.

'Hey.'

'So you bought the black one?'

'Yes. Though I feel I may regret it. My husband doesn't like Western dresses too much.'

'Oh, I love it when my wife wears such stuff' he said, adding for good measure, 'I positively encourage it!'

'What do you think of this?' He showed her a necklace that he had been admiring the last few minutes.

She furrowed her brow and he felt encouraged by the attention she was devoting to it.

'Lovely! Your wife is lucky to have a husband who shops for her…'

'Ha ha, I try not to make a habit of it. I just have a break between meetings. So, is it approved?'

'But now you have to help me search for cuff links for my husband.'

'I can try, but I'm afraid I'll be useless. I've never worn cuff links in my life.'

'Don't worry, just tell me whether you like them or not.'

'What do you think of these?' He picked up a pair which had an unusual shape.

'Oh, very nice,' she said and her eyes lit up. Her fingers touched his as she took them from his hands. He noticed that they lingered.

'You have very good taste,' she commented as they settled their bills.

'Lunch? Coffee? Some wine?' he asked as they made their way towards the escalators.

'No. Aaj mera fast hai. Shivji ka. I can give you company,' though.

■

Within fifteen minutes, a record by any standard, they have skipped the pleasantries and the conversation has turned to sex. They compare frequencies. He complains about his wife's once-a-week quota.

'He's travelling all the time. And the rare days when he's at home, all he wants to do is sleep, sit with his parents or watch TV. You guys have a dream sex life compared to mine,' she says. 'I never thought marriage could be so lonely; the only reason I wanted to get married was the companionship. We used to spend hours on the phone talking.'

She toys with the salt and pepper shakers moodily, checking him out when she thinks he isn't looking. 'He's not like you. He's really let himself go. He doesn't play any sport, he doesn't exercise. It's just about how many billable hours to the client and how many Hugo Boss suits. And he sleeps so much.' She pours some salt on her hand and licks it. 'I never knew a human being could sleep as much. I lie awake like an idiot all the time. But,' she leans forward conspiratorially and drops her voice, 'I've discovered new ways to masturbate.'

She catches his glance straying towards her cleavage, looks him in the eye and makes no effort to cover up. 'I've even watched porn. I can't watch more than a few minutes at one time, though. I don't know how you men watch it for hours. The worst part is that I know even he watches it. I've seen some of his hotel bills abroad. But with me, nothing. No action at all.' She leans back and toys with her pendant.

'I know I'm attractive, men do look at me, I get a lot of attention when we go out to parties. But our circle is very boring. No one like you in the fashion industry, designing stuff, creative stuff!' She leans forward again, at an angle this time and he can swear that she chooses it so that more of her is visible.

'I would love to make love to you,' she whispers again, 'but I can't do this whole hotel room thing. It would be cheap and I wouldn't be comfortable. But I would really, really love to have some good sex!'

He looks steadily at her.

'I could figure something out.' He holds her hand and draws her close, kissing her tenderly on her forehead.

'Come, let's go for a walk,' he says as he pulls her up and they leave, their drinks untouched, their arms are around each other.

He has no concrete plan, just a rough idea as they walk around the mall on the level below the food court. He steals a few kisses when no one is looking. His eyes light up when he sees the multiplex but as he walks towards it, she shakes her head and gently guides him away.

'I don't think I could do it in a public place,' she says.

That's when he sees the La Senza store. From previous experience, he knows that the store has very few customers and is struggling for sales. He also knows that the staff works on commission. He looks inside the store, sees that there is only one assistant, likes the look of her and walks in with Yellow Dress holding his hand tightly.

He begins with his most winning smile. 'Hi, I have an unusual request to make.'

He gestures at Yellow Dress. 'She wants to shop for lingerie and wants me to approve. But she is too shy to come out dressed only in this.' He points around to the stuff on display.

'But, sir, there is no one there, ma'am shouldn't feel uncomfortable.'

He responds by looking behind, over his shoulder, where the glass windows of the shop ensures that everything inside is visible even to the casual passerby.

'But, sir, what can we do?'

'Look,' he moves a little closer, flashing his winning smile once more, 'let me go with her inside the trial room. She will bring all the stuff she wants to try inside with her. When we're done, we'll come out.'

He knows she will refuse so he throws in the clincher. 'We

promise to buy at least ten items from you.'

The shop assistant is now all smiles.

'Of course, sir, no problem.'

She waits till there is no one outside the store window and then ushers him in. Yellow Dress takes a few minutes picking up stuff to try and then follows, hesitating outside the curtains of the trial rooms, trying to figure out which one to use. He drags her in, straight into his arms, and their lips meet, hungry for each other. The cubicle has a small sofa bench fitted against the wall.

He sits down, with her on top of him, the lingerie carelessly flung aside. She begins undoing his shirt buttons while they are still kissing, moving quickly. He has his arms around her and is slowly inching her dress above her waist when she impatiently stands up for a few seconds, pulls her dress off, unhooks her bra and sits down again on him, offering her left breast to his lips. His mouth alternates between her lips and breasts, while his hands focused on discovering the inner recesses of her panties. After a minute or so, she stands up again and removes her panties, while he removes his jeans and briefs.

This time he sits down at an angle to help her place her knees on the narrow sofa and guide his penis inside her. They are both completely ready for each other, kissing fiercely and after a while she leans her head back, just a little, her eyes closed, her breathing increasing bit by bit. She takes his hands and guides them to her buttocks, making him squeeze them hard.

'Oh… Oh…!' She now digs her nails into his shoulders, rocking back and forth as much as she can in the constricted space. She comes soon, her mouth wide open, her breathing silent but heavy, surprise writ large on her face. Her forehead, her back, her shoulders are bathed in sweat. Neither of them has bothered switching on the tiny fan in the corner. She looks at him lovingly, kisses him gently and then begins to rock herself again, this time her hands going for his buttocks, sliding under them. She kisses him on the neck, on the shoulders, on his chest, murmuring, 'You're so hard, you smell so good.' They come together, and both of them orgasm longer and more intensely than they have even done before.

He warns her, telling her to lift up and away so that he can come outside her, but she grips him tightly and presses her knees against him even tighter, forcing him to spurt inside her.

She nestles her head against his shoulders and breathes deeply, kissing him again before getting up. She has finished dressing even as he buttons his shirt up. When he gets up, she hugs him tightly before scooping up the untried lingerie and walking out. The tab is his, of course, and once the payment is made, they walk out hand in hand. Their first stop is a pharmacy in the mall where she buys an i-pill and washes it down with some bottled water. She then pecks him on the cheek, hands him the bag of lingerie and walks away, never once looking back.

■

They only met once again ever, in the same mall, purely by chance. They walked in again to La Senza and were relieved to see the same shop assistant. She gave them a knowing smile, held up the fingers of both her hands and, on receiving his confirmatory nod, held the curtain for the trial room open for them to enter.

The Bike Ride

Eleven p.m. She needed to get to Manesar, fifty kilometres from the flat in Kamla Nagar which she shared with a classmate. It took her an hour of cajoling and emotional blackmail to convince him to drop her off. He wasn't being lazy. It was just that he was very sleepy and didn't trust himself to remain awake. However, they were soon on the Ring Road, zooming past the Interstate Bus Terminus, on their way to National Highway 8.

They had been together for sixteen months, having been drawn to each other from the first time they met in Hansraj College, Delhi University. He was bearded, slightly plump, bedraggled in dress but amiable in disposition. She was short, dusky and freckled, in-between plump and thin, but had amazingly sharp features and lovely, intelligent eyes which lit up every time she spoke about something she felt deeply about.

The entire college thought that they were a couple and, in most senses, they were. They took most decisions jointly, and had even planned their second-year courses in order to be able to maximize time with each other. But they didn't move in. They had sometimes stayed over at each other's houses, but this was for logistical reasons rather than romantic ones. They knew that the entire college thought they were doing it, but they did not care too much either way. Their relationship had, apart from a few kisses, remained platonic.

Had they been asked, neither would've been able to explain why it was so. They were comfortable with each other, content to sit for hours, talking. He had tried to initiate sex a few times in the initial months. And while she hadn't been ready the first couple of times, something or the other had happened the other few. He had never tried again after that, content that things would happen when they would happen.

She had initiated things once or twice as well but he had gently refused. She had had a few drinks both times and he was a thorough gentleman.

■

Sex was the furthest thing on his mind when they crossed the toll plaza on the Gurgaon-Delhi Expressway. Sleep buffeted him in gusts, and took over his brain and his eyelids. Luckily, there was hardly any traffic and he continued to soldier on gamely. She made him pull over at a roadside dhaba just next to the Sohna Road turning, bought some chips and Pepsi, holding the bottle while he sipped. When they set off again, she clutched him tightly. She could not strike up a conversation, the sound of the bike and the noise of the traffic on the highway was too loud. She tried to get him to listen to music from her phone, and tried to fit the earphones into his ears, but he shrugged them off. If he did fall asleep, the sound of an oncoming horn was most likely to save him and he couldn't risk being deafened by music when that happened. However, the bike soon wobbled again, and this time she knew stronger remedies would be required.

She pressed against his bulk and felt her breasts being squished—she enjoyed the feeling. She began to rub her hands over his chest, softly at first and then a little firmly. He remained impassive but she noticed in the rearview mirror that his eyes were now awake. After a few minutes, she slipped her hands under his windcheater and over his T-shirt. Then a few minutes later, she slipped under that and gently massaged his chest. The bike wobbled again, but this time it happened because she had pulled at the hair on his chest. She now began playing with his nipples, first rubbing them, then cupping them, then circling them with her thumbs and, finally, pinching them with her fingers.

She pulled her hands out, brought them close to her face and inhaled his smell and his warmth. She licked both her hands and then slid them carefully back in, using her nails where possible to hold the T-shirt up as the hands made their way back towards his nipples. She wanted to save the wetness for his nipples. It had the desired effect, making him gasp slightly when her fingers reached their intended destination. A slow sigh of pleasure escaped his lips as her fingers again began to massage his chest and they continued to do so for the next fifteen minutes, with only some momentary pit-stops to ensure that her fingers remained wet.

The next wobble, a big one, came when she lifted herself up slightly and kissed the nape of his neck, burying her face in his thick crop of hair. He cleared his throat once he had regained control of the bike and she resumed her kisses, now spreading them generously on his ears, his bearded cheeks and the side of his neck. Her hands and lips began to move in tandem now, oblivious to the disbelieving hoots from the few cars and trucks passing them. The bike speed had now dropped considerably, his mind obviously on other things.

Ready for the next step, she sat back comfortably on the bike, pressing her own firm, aroused breasts hard against him again. Her hands made their way around his waist, unbuckled his belt, unclasped his jeans and unzipped his fly. The bike wobbled again, but he quickly brought the bike to the straight and the narrow once more. She noticed, though, that the speed had reduced even more significantly now. Encouraged by this, her hands burrowed inside his open zip, seeking his penis. She wasn't surprised to find it erect. She brought a hand back to her mouth, licked it lavishly, and then returned it to his crotch. He had a big dick, she knew, but she hadn't realized that it was quite so massive; she was holding it with both hands and there was still some unclaimed territory. She now began to work on the tip, using her fingers to tease it, touch it, coax it to greater heights. The frequency of her pulling her hands back to wet them also increased and she was now doing it almost every sixth or seventh stroke. She burrowed the other hand deeper inside his boxers, finding his balls and giving them a gentle massage as well, while one hand remained firmly on his penis.

It seemed like a very long time, but couldn't have been more than a few minutes after which she felt his penis begin to throb in her hands. She continued stroking—base upwards—with one hand and still touching the tip with the other. In a few seconds more, he ejaculated. The bike was moving at a snail's pace now, but so were her hands. She continued to stroke his penis with her left hand while it throbbed and spat its juice into the other. She carried on stroking long after he had come. Then she lifted her right hand, full of cum, uncurled her fingers and let the wind blow it all away. She kept both of her hands outstretched and her eyes closed for a few miles, wondering why her own heart was beating so fast, why she was feeling so thrilled.

They entered the city limits of Manesar, their destination, and she awkwardly began to zip him up and button him again. Then they both began to laugh. Slowly at first but then louder, she holding him, he putting one hand behind, clutching her in an awkward embrace. They arrived at her home a few minutes later, she got off and pecked him on the cheek and rushed inside, smiling and blushing furiously. He, without stopping the engine, just turned around and began his journey back. Fully awake and with a big smile plastered on his face.

■

They made love properly as soon as she returned. And moved into the same flat a few days later. The neighbours sometimes complain to each other about the bed which creaks late at night but the couple is so sweet and so inoffensive that no one can hold a grudge against them for too long.

Confessions of an IPL Escort

Tina lay naked on her bed, absent-mindedly running her hands over her body, thinking of her fetish for cricket and cricketers. As she idly caressed herself, she decided to masturbate. She looked at the full-length mirror on the wall. If she propped her head up on a pillow, she could see her entire body. After she had adjusted her position and was comfortably settled, her mind turned to the past and the events which had brought her to this lovely flat in Mumbai, and this magnificent view of the Arabian Sea.

■

Tina was born in Saharanpur, a small town in Uttar Pradesh. She had been so stunningly beautiful from a very young age that people wondered if her dull-looking parents had actually begotten her. Tina had always dreamed of a brighter life but the small-town realities of life ground her down and suffocated her. At the end of her school years, Tina made two resolutions: one, to escape Saharanpur; two, to marry a cricketer. The next two years, which she spent attending college, became a succession of fights with her parents, unending proposals of marriage and a series of indecent advances made by the boys and men of her town.

Then Dev came into her life; the man who had got her out of Saharanpur. A cricketer in the employ of a big domestic airline, Dev used to work as a flight attendant when not playing matches. He had a good-looking wife and a son he doted on. When he had first asked her why she didn't apply for a job with the airline, she had thought he was joking.

Even though she had dealt with men from her early teenage years, Dev's rather direct proposal had shocked Tina. He had invited her to office to fill out a job application form. (The office turned out to be Dev's friend's flat.) In the office, Dev put forward his proposal in a very direct, businesslike manner, calling the exchange their 'arrangement'. He would get her a job, her escape from small-town Saharanpur to the big, beautiful world waiting outside. In return, he wanted sex on demand.

The sex, when it happened, had turned out to be as businesslike as their arrangement. Foreplay was not really his thing. Including a quick phone call to co-ordinate timings, Dev would usually be in and out within fifteen minutes. His preferred position was missionary, and apart from his habit of coming all over her, especially on her breasts, everything else about the sex was unmemorable. She had attended a few matches he played in and had realized that he would never progress beyond the small leagues. Their jobs, thankfully, had entailed a lot of travel and calendar co-ordination had not been easy.

■

Tina was having trouble arousing herself. And the memories of Dev didn't help, either. She shifted her hands from her nipples to her pubic hair and began caressing it, inching her way south. That reminded her of Sumit.

Sumit, or seat number 2F, as she recalled, had been very different from all the other men in her life. He had genuinely cared about her. A cricketer for the Rajasthan Ranji team, he was employed by the Indian Oil Corporation in a cushy manager-level role. He travelled a lot but didn't do much actual work.

One of the few demands Sumit made of Tina was that she let her pubic hair grow out. He would lie with his head nestling amidst her curls, making good use of his rough, lean, strong spinner's fingers. He could bring her to climax over and over again, making up for his small cannon with enthusiasm and technique. He always made sure her orgasms had as many revolutions per minute as some of his off-breaks.

Using some of his contacts, he had got her a bit part in a film song sequence. She—and he—had thought this was it. That was supposed to have been her big break, the first step in her inevitable rise to stardom. By then she had been a flight attendant for a year and a half. After eighteen months of picking up vomit bags, assisting elderly ladies as they peed in cramped toilets, lifting heavy bags for rude business-class folks and fending off advances from all and sundry, Tina had decided enough was enough. She had quit, moved in with Sumit, and had devoted her energies to try and make her film career work.

When the bit part was eventually edited out of the film, Sumit held her hands through the heartbreak. He had tried to get her more roles and even succeeded a few times, but they had mostly been the seventh-dancer-in-the-third-row kind of stuff. Tina remained undiscovered.

Then the Indian Premier League had taken off, which both Sumit and Tina were sure would propel them to unimaginable riches and glory. But Sumit, deemed a better Test player than a T20 one, had remained unsold. It shattered his confidence. He lost his job, his place in the Ranji team and his flat in Mumbai. She did the best she could and tried to egg him on, but he was past caring. He became slowly consumed by drink, and was unable to even achieve an erection on most days.

■

The thoughts of the spinner's fingers had been just thing Tina needed. She rubbed furiously with three fingers, both her long legs aloft in ecstasy. At the moment, she needed just the right visual to tip herself over the edge. Which is when she thought of darling Shawn.

Shawn was by far the richest and most flamboyant guy she had ever known. He was also the best lover she had ever had, both in terms of his technique and the range of experimentation he was willing to indulge in. He really knew how to give a girl a good time. Shawn was a cricketer from Australia playing for one of the IPL teams but, after a disappointing first season on the field and several unsavoury incidents off it, he had been told in no uncertain terms that he would not be playing for the franchise again. He was receiving his full payment, though, and would travel with the team, live the high life, and attend all the parties. Given his infectious energy, his sexual appetites and commercial bent of mind, Shawn was soon running Mumbai's best, most expensive and most exclusive escort service. He had the perfect contacts, attended the right parties, was privy to inside information like no one else; he also had a direct line to the IPL cheerleaders.

Shawn had spotted Tina at a pricey mall in Mumbai, ogling some expensive lingerie and had gallantly bought it for her. The obligatory coffee had led to an obligatory dinner and the obligatory drinks and lovemaking at his place. God! The feel of the bed linen, the furry, soft quilts and the lacy negligee he had bought her had been almost enough to make her come by themselves. But it had Shawn's skill with his hands, his tongue and, finally, with his throbbing cock, which had made her come in wave after exhausting wave. She had stopped counting her orgasms by the third one and just lay back, her mouth open, letting the ecstasy wash over her.

The memory of her first climax with Shawn was enough to push her over. The intense orgasm brought instant relief to the headache which had been her constant companion since morning. Coffee is highly overrated, she thought to herself, as she got up and held the dress she had selected for the evening against her body, admiring herself in the mirror. It was a big night. She was one of Shaun's girls now and he had got her a gig in one of the top after-parties of the IPL.

■

When Tina reached the venue, Shawn came over and hugged her. He whispered into his ear that this was a big night for her. Shawn made it a point to not sleep too often with any of his girls, a habit which had held him in good stead. It kept the girls under check and didn't let the personal interfere too much with the professional. This way, the girls were also more than happy to sleep with him when he wanted them to. No one knew how many girls he ran. But given that Shawn did not retain any girl beyond two years, no one really knew.

Shawn introduced Tina to Mathew, the concierge of the posh hotel the players were staying at, and also the venue of the party. Mathew looked her up and down in lecherous approval, made a V-for-victory sign with his fingers to Shawn and took her inside into a smaller, more intimate room. The party for the general public was being held in the ballroom. This seemed like a conference room; a table for eight occupied centre stage. In one corner, a well-stocked bar had been laid out. It was a Grey Goose, Blue Label kind of bar, and she had one of each as she waited for the players to arrive. Mathew tried to keep talking to her and impress her with his own importance, but she zoned out completely after her third drink. She perked up briefly when he mentioned something about the rate being fixed with Shawn at one lakh rupees per—but then she zoned out again.

One lakh was at the lower end of what she was used to earning per night, but Shawn handled the commercials for all his girls, and he never cheated them out of the fifty per cent that was their share. So the question of speaking about rates, especially with someone as smarmy as Mathew, just did not arise. She was a few drinks down and quite content to wait for the other girls who would surely arrive.

Five players walked in. Tina's heart skipped a beat. She had always found the skipper of this team a bit of a hottie. His recent marriage had not reduced his sex appeal one bit, in her humble opinion. The tall South African who was accompanying him was rumoured to possess the ability to go on well past conventional human limits. And the other three were reserve players. They all were very polite, the men, and the reserve players made sure to always stay a few steps behind the first-team regulars as they chatted with her. The players' drinks arrived without them having to ask for them.

The skipper made the first move. In the middle of their conversation—about his two monstrous sixes in the day's match—he leaned across and kissed her. She took an involuntary step back, surprised. She had been steeling herself, thinking that she had been chosen for the local lad, one of the reserves, who had finally got a game today and had acquitted himself well. The captain, recently married, she had thought was off the market.

She recovered admirably, though. Cooing cutely, she mumbled sweet somethings about him being forceful and putting her arm around his waist, planted a firm, wet kiss on his mouth. The South African now came back, stood behind her and lifted up her dress even as she kissed the skipper. He then lifted her up, gently placed her on her back on the conference table and entered her. But not before she had seen the size of his thing and gasped.

The skipper moved around the table, continuing to kiss her, and lifted her dress over the breasts, kissing them as well. His South African mate was moving like a piston. Thoughts of how she had never done it with someone else watching, and about charging extra, crossed her mind. But every time the man pumped, he drove every thought away from her mind and it was all she could do to control the involuntary groans which escaped her. He came very quickly though. His near-mythical ability to go on for hours was just that: a myth.

The skipper then invited the three reserves to take position. Tina looked at him, eyes wide open, unsure whether to carry on or bring the proceedings to a stop. He sensed her hesitation and quickly whipped out his phone, dialled a number and spoke abruptly, 'The deal with her was for all of us, right?' He presumably heard what he wanted to hear for he soon returned his full attention to her breasts even as the three took their turn one by one. After the second reserve had pumped himself dry, she lost all sensation down there. As she looked down at the head of the skipper—one of her childhood idols—now nestled between her breasts, nuzzling her skin, she wondered if this was what it all boiled down to.

He's a good team player, Tina thought to herself, and puts the team before self. Perhaps that was why his squad was so loyal to him. Just when she was thinking if the skipper would have a go as well, he stopped slurping at her breasts and asked, 'Why don't you get cleaned up?' By then, the third reserve had spent himself and was again standing at a respectful distance from the regulars.

As she straightened her dress and left, he told everyone to clear out, even the barman. When she returned, the lights had been turned off and the illumination from the party next door, now in full swing, was just sufficient to make out his silhouette and register the fact that they were alone.

She sat on the table, spread her legs, and pulled him towards herself. She undressed him swiftly, professionally. She could see that the wait had whetted his appetite; he was ready for her. Though she had had four already that evening, when he entered her, she moaned in pure pleasure. The sound excited him and he increased his pace. He began to grunt, too, but after a little while, his pace began to flag, though the enthusiasm remained undimmed. Oh no, she thought, buddy boy needs to go to the gym more often. He gripped her shoulders and propping himself thus, began to pump slowly but with force. She used her hands to ruffle his curly hair, his neck and the hair on his chest. He came inside her with a shudder and she gripped his buttocks, determined to take him in deep. He rolled over beside her, spent, silent. After a couple of minutes, he dressed up and walked out without saying a word. After a few more minutes, she walked out, too, her eyes squinting in the sudden glare of the lights, trying to adjust to the deafening sounds of the party.

Mathew walked up to her, leering obscenely. He said, 'Hi! How was it?'

She just looked silently at him.

'That good, huh,' he said, chortling at his own wit. 'Come, we'll be paying you in cash. Is that cool?' He led her through the crowd to a clutch of rooms. As she walked behind him, she hoped that he wasn't trying to pull a fast one, that he wouldn't make any advances. She wouldn't be able to handle it tonight. He knocked on a closed door, which opened almost instantly.

She recognized the man inside as the scion of one of the more prominent families which dealt in gutka and real estate. The cricketers were all regulars at their parties and she now put two and two together. He said 'Namaste, miss,' very politely and led her inside, offering her a drink which she politely refused. He then handed over bundles of one lakh rupees each one by one. 'Madam, yeh one…two…three…four…' and, with an air of finality, 'five.' She debated asking for something extra, for giving the others the pleasure of watching while one made love to her, but then decided to drop it. The gutka kid seemed nice. He was smiling broadly at her and she wasn't sure why.

He then dipped his hand in his cash bag once more. 'Aur yeh one…two…three…four…five.' He placed five more bundles in front of her, 'Captaan sahib bole hain, khaas aapke liye, bonus.' He beamed. Mathew's eyes were almost popping out of their sockets. He clearly wasn't privy to this and that made Tina almost as happy as the unexpected bonus.

'Are you sure you'll be fine with all this cash?' Mathew asked, his hands moving towards the new heap. She quickly scooped it all up before he could get any ideas.

The gallant gutka scion came to her rescue again. 'Madam, neeche, gaadi number twenty-three thirty-four. Red Mercedes. Driver aapko chhod dega.' She needed no second invitation to leave, Mathew scrambling after her. She knew that he wanted a piece of the bonus or her ass and was determined to keep both to herself.

Once outside the door, he said, 'Sorry about all that cash. These guys are all rolling in black money, so they pay all their endorsement amounts in cash.'

She decided it was time to shed the bastard. She turned on her best fake smile, said, 'Thanks Mathew, I'll carry on from here,' shook his hand and walked out.

■

A couple of weeks later, Shawn, who seemed to be buzzing, called her. 'Yo babe,' he said, 'you've done some magic on our man. The skipper wants you again, if you're up for it.'

After two delectable rendezvous, the skipper got her a job as

Chief Purser in his private jet—paid for by one of his sponsors, of course.

Well, she isn't married to a cricketer, but sees more of one of India's most famous cricketers than his wife does. And, she is sure she fucks him more frequently too.

■

Sexting: Fast and Furious

01:31 Hi!

01:32 Hi! Beautiful Bong babe!

01:32 What are you up to? Are you at home?

01:32 Yep. So when are we meeting?

01:33 Don't know, yeah! Work is keeping me busy.

01:33 Damn! I was looking forward to it. You have no time for the men in your life. You've heard what they say: 'All work and no play can make Jill very gay!' ☺

01:34 Hee Hee! C'mon, I always have time for you... ☹

01:34 Want to plan something for end April? Some place near the sea?

01:34 Not sure. Does May first week work? Know for sure hubby is travelling then. ☺

01:35 Nope. Have to attend family wedding with wife and kids. ☹ Later?

01:35 Oh, never mind! What would you do with me right now?

01:35 Right now?

01:36 YES! You know, I always regret not doing it with you, especially when we had that chance.

01:36 Me too. But ma'am, I'll need some visual stimulation before I can respond appropriately.

01:37 <Image Sent>

01:37 Onek! Beshi! Bhalo!

01:38 Giggle. For a Haryanvi Jat, your Bangla isn't bad.

01:38 Completely inspired by your stunning landscape. Always been partial to hills and valleys ☺!!!

01:38 So what would you do with me? Right now?

01:39 Right now, a leisurely soak in a jacuzzi with you would just hit the spot.

01:39 How about some wine? And not necessarily in the glass…☺

01:40 Yes, some rainfall in the hills and valleys would be great.

01:40 It's all part of the jacuzzi service. Champagne for drinking, wine for flooding…

01:41 Just looked at your photo again. I think your breasts lend themselves wonderfully to wine…

01:41 So, in the jacuzzi, what would you do?

01:42 Sit behind you, my legs wrapped around you, and give you a thorough scrub with my hands.

01:42 When you've had enough back-scrubbing, turn you around and have you sit on top of me. Your legs wrapped around mine. And carry on as long as needed.

01:42 Does that meet your approval?

01:42 Makes me wet!

01:42 Tell me some more!!

01:43 I will focus on your nipples, thighs, and your pussy with my hand.

01:43 And only when you're nearing orgasm will I enter.

01:44 Kiss my nipples?

01:44 And bite them hard…

01:44 But only after I'm inside you.

01:44 You're a teaser? Play with them at least? They hate being left out.

01:45 My hands would ensure they never feel left out.

01:45 What would you do to me?

01:45 Let this be about me.

01:45 Tonight, I want you to love my body!

01:46 Talk to me, burn me up!!!!

01:46 Kisses, when I'm in, on the back of the neck, on your pubic hair. Fingers loving your anus gently.

01:47 Slap your cock against my pussy. Rub against it.

01:47 I'll spread your legs, raise them high in the air while I fuck you.

1:48 Savage my breasts. Your fingers playing with my clitoris. Your tongue on my nipples. And you in my hand.

01:48 I would like to go down on you, make you come that way, before entering you.

01:48 Yesss…

01:48 Confident in my ability to make you come again after I enter.

01:48 Yesss…

01:48 Want to feel your cock throb in my hands.

01:49 Want to hear you moan loudly. Fuck you hard!

01:49 Make you orgasm again and again!! And keep fucking you while you come!!

01:49 Yesssss!

01:49 Want to sleep with you inside me.

01:49 Will pump you like a machine.

01:49 Do you like the taste of cum?

01:50 ??

01:51 Hello???

01:55 Oye!!??

02:01 NOT FAIR!!!!!

08:32 Slept like a baby. Thanks for last night. Don't they say all's fair in LOVE AND WAR?

09:15 @##$$ Will show you what's fair and not when we meet. Revenge will be mine!!

Dear Neanderthal

Dear Neanderthal,

'Man'-kind's intelligence has always puzzled me. I simply cannot understand how the minds which discovered penicillin and electricity; invented the iPod and the television; and created wonders such as *Calvin and Hobbes* can be so limited when it comes to dealing with the female of your species. More specifically, the one whom you are married to?

I know your love for to-do lists, my dear. So I am going to make one for you. And as ticking off the boxes in this checklist will directly affect how much you will get laid, I suggest you PAY ATTENTION.

1. Sports

NO, SPORTS DON'T TURN ME ON. Not unless they are the kind that you intend to play with me. When I am feeling horny, I don't want to hear that I must 'hold that thought' for fifteen minutes while you watch the last over of the match being bowled or the last ten minutes of the soccer half play out. I don't care that you are watching the World Cup or the European Cup which come around only after years. When I am in the mood, darling, all I care about is one of your hands cupping my breast even as the other is showing my clitoris a good time.

Remember darling, no woman wants to play second fiddle to anyone. Me, least of all. (I could go on and on about how you run to answer, sometimes even in the middle of sex, when your mom calls, but that is part of another checklist.) See, if you prefer to put sports ahead of me on your priority list, that is fine with me. But I will demote you, too, to behind chocolates, diamonds, handbags—even shoes.

The next time you begin to paw me as soon as your sports match has ended, even though I've just fallen asleep, do so with the knowledge that I am well within my rights to kill you. And given that just fifteen minutes earlier you had been seeing right through me, not stopping once to admire the expensive, thoughtfully chosen lingerie or even acknowledging my horniness, I don't think any judge could ever convict me for avenging such blatant disregard. Especially when she considers that the reason for your distraction are over-paid athletes prancing around in laughably tight clothes, chasing balls either small or large.

2. Maintain Personal Hygiene:

If you touch me once more after having picked your nose or scratched your balls or licked your fingers to get the 'last taste of curry', I will have to devise new methods of torture for you. WASH YOUR HANDS. And no, not just with water; use soap.

The fact that I wax, tweeze, thread, exfoliate and perform a few more painful yet necessary actions in the interest of personal hygiene and your aesthetic pleasure should act as a sufficient hint for you, but it obviously doesn't. (You know, I always bear in mind your preference that I keep my bush trimmed but you, on the other hand, are like some tropical jungle. After every time you ask me for oral pleasure, I have to gargle just to get the hair out from between my teeth. PLEASE TRIM.)

Never kiss me without having brushed and no, I don't find the lingering taste of burnt tobacco on your tongue sexy. In fact, it makes me want to gag.

3. Say Something Nice

When was the last time you paid me a compliment? Think back and remember if we had sex that night. Do you get my drift? When I am complimented, I feel appreciated and that releases certain endorphins which compel me to do things I normally wouldn't. I can look away from the paunch which you have begun to ignore and in which, I suspect, you even take a little pride. The endorphins take my attention away from your thinning hair and even your silly, juvenile jokes seem funny. (I mean, you haven't still moved beyond sad little fart jokes.)

I do a million things everyday and even just a small word of appreciation would make me feel that it was worth it. I mean, laundry doesn't just happen by itself. I can't conjure meals with a single clap.

And a whole lot of effort and deliberation goes into making me look the way I do. So hot that even after so many years, I can simply run my hand down your fly and you become rock hard.

If you feel the need to say something nice and genuine, say it. I am not telepathic.

4. Repeat, 'Mental, too, Not Just Physical.'
You, who are guided solely by the dictates of your joystick, must remember this specially. The next time you slip your hand down the front of my panties check if I am ready, without having revved me up, everything stops rights there.

Set the mood. Show me that you care. That I mean something. There is an eight-letter word which I want you to learn by heart: f-o-r-e-p-l-a-y.

Okay, let me explain this in words you will understand. Think of it as the playoffs with no final. Or like collecting the $200 in Monopoly before passing Go, which will send you to to Jail. In short, if you try to score a goal without dribbling and passing and being a team man, you might end up having to score an own goal.

5. Remember, Everything Is Connected
Again, this is tough to explain to a man who finds it difficult to sustain a single thought in his head for more than three seconds. I am a creature of the mind (as explained above) and everything for me is inter-connected.

If you've yelled at me during the day—it doesn't really matter whose fault it was. Or have made some disparaging remark about me appearance. Or have ignored me through the day. Or chosen not to allow me to vent on how my day has been (extra negative points if you've used management jargon, phrases such as 'Deal with it!' or 'That's your department!'). Or if the house is a mess.

Or if the kids have fever. Or if you've forced me to watch some action flick. Remember, Everything adds up.

And no amount of porn can put me in the mood if even one of the above has taken place. Just because I got wet one time watching that hot couple go at it doesn't mean porn will work every time. In fact, I don't know how you can watch it all the damn time.

If you really want to change the mood, you'll have to work harder than just surfing porn on the Internet. Get me a gift— the sparklier the better. Make a thoughtful gesture: help with the chores, stop discussing my in-laws with me, light some scented candles at bedtime, get me some flowers, chocolates and, for a change, go with my choice of wine instead of yours. Else, chances are that I might just get a permanent headache.

6. Warmth

This last point is a tip. Only in movies do women writhe in feverish arousal when the man rubs ice on her naked body. I hate it. Look at this way. You have a rock-hard erection, as big and hard as you can ever get. You come to me. I wrap my hands around your cock, but they are both sheets of ice. Result: your hard rock becomes a raisin. Warmth is good; both in the way you talk to me as well as in the room when we make love. The AC has to be set just right in the summer, and we should have sheets to cover us in winter. There isn't much I wouldn't do to you if you only have the foresight to rub your hands before putting them on me.

Your slightly peeved but still loving,
Wife

At the Big Fat Indian Wedding

The Opportunity

- Aditya, thirty-two, single, has three 'new' potential liaisons lined up for the upcoming weekend wedding.

Situation Analysis

- Rohan, his cousin, best friend and erstwhile partner in crime, is getting married to Aaliya after a three-month-long 'whirlwind' romance.
- The wedding is being organized in an exclusive resort. All seventy-five rooms of the resort have been reserved for the marriage.
- The resort, in Lonavala, is situated on top of a mountain peak. The last three kilometres up to the resort is a dirt track. No mobile network is available.

The Acquisition Targets

- Meghna: The most exciting candidate, Aaliya's 'best friend'. She has categorically told Rohan that she is available in case things didn't work out with Aaliya. That offer has zoomed her up the charts in Aditya's fuck-list.

- Urvi: Number two on the list. She is six years younger to Aditya and has a figure to die for, even though it is mostly camouflaged by non-revealing salwar-kameezes. She has just reconnected with him after many years, at an airport, of all places. Urvi had recognized him and had approached him herself. She had seemed very impressed by the way he effortlessly got her into the Executive Lounge, by his business class ticket, and by the Cosmopolitan he had got the barman to mix for her. From the texts he gets from her which are variations of 'having a Cosmopolitan, thinking of you', he fears that he has either started her on the road to alcoholism or she has cornered the North Indian market for Cosmos. She has made it clear that she isn't close to Rohan, she only wants to spend time with him. He, on the other hand, is quite certain that she doesn't have sex on her mind but, given an opportunity, he is also certain that he can change her mind.

- Sabah: Possibility number three. Their families had been neighbours for a few years when they were both young. He still vividly remembers the exciting explorations of their teenage years. They had lost touch over time until recently, when she had got in touch on Facebook. He had found that she was still sexy after many years and two children. And based on their FB chats, he could tell that she had lost none of her spunk.

Success Criteria

- Three new conquests over the weekend will make him worthy of the Stud Hall of Fame.
- Two will be great for his ego which has taken a battering after a recent dry spell.
- One would be, well, better than none, but it would carry the lingering fragrance of under-achievement around it.
- None. He will say yes to the first woman his long-suffering parents parade past him.

Constraints

- No mobile reception, no SMS means that co-ordination in the sprawling resort will be difficult.
- All the singles are sharing rooms, the walls of which are made of flimsy material. He can hear his elderly uncle in the next room watch FTV. His parents are squabbling in the other adjoining room. The logistics of getting a soundproof, unoccupied room is clearly going to be a challenge worthy of his managerial skills.
- The weather is lovely, misty and very romantic, but also very wet. Which means that the great outdoors aren't really for the heavily made-up Indian women who are born and brought up indoors. He knows a couple of Russian and German women for whom the weather wouldn't have been a problem at all, but Indians seem to be made out of of salt and are scared of rainwater.
- His parents arrived at the wedding having made up their minds to finally hitch him up. His mother had had a steely look in her eyes when she had asked the receptionist to give her the room next to his.

- Urvi and Sabah stepped off the bus arm in arm. If they are friends, bedding both over the weekend will be potentially fraught with danger. Akin to picking daisies in a minefield.

- Meghna is hotter than he had ever imagined. Her legs promise pleasures he has not yet experienced, her lithe figure promises sex which will be off the Richter scale, and her fashion sense—plunging necklines and ascending hemlines—screams, 'If you've got it, flaunt it.' But she seems to be sticking too close to Aaliya and is still eyeing Rohan. This will clearly have to be dealt with.

- Last, but in no ways the least, Rohan is a nervous wreck. The enormity of what he is about to do hits him like a sledgehammer and reduces him to something just above a jellyfish on the evolutionary scale. He is clinging to Aditya and wants him around all the time.

Let the Games Begin

Aditya decided to focus on Meghna first; Urvi was slotted next and Sabah is third. He did this strictly in order of the probability of success, taking the saying, 'a bird in the hand is worth two in the bush' to its logical conclusion.

He persuaded Meghna to come on a trek with him, envisioning a nice, relaxed, romantic time together amongst lush green environs. The first hint that things were not going according to plan came when she invited fifteen other people along. Meghna also turned out to be one of those fitness fiends. Apparently, treadmills and assorted StairMasters burned out under her feet with alarming regularity. Aditya, recently back from a holiday to the great Punjab, with multiple parathas, dal makhnis and butter chickens under his stealthily expanding girth, was hopelessly unprepared for anything more than a gentle stroll.

Meghna, though, having been told by an amiable local guide that he normally did the trek to a nearby lake in forty-five minutes, was determined to beat the record. She and another ridiculously fit friend of hers were already on their way back when the remainder of the expedition had just reached halfway there. Hands on knees, bent over, Aditya gazed wistfully at her rapidly retreating rear as she disappeared from view.

Aditya returned to the resort a broken man, both in spirit and in body. The walk back was particularly strenuous and the final fifteen minutes of vertical ascent took a great toll on him. When he asked for Meghna, he was told that she had gone to the gym to warm down. He decided to warm down in the traditional way. He picked up a bottle of rum and made his way to his room

His room-mate turned out to be another cousin. One of the nerdy IIM-A types. A banker who was interested more in money than what it can buy. The kind who is cited as an example to all those kids who don't study enough (i.e. 99.9 per cent of all kids). One look at him studiously poring over *The Economics Times* was enough to make him do a quick U-turn.

In dire need of sympathy, he sought Urvi but was waylaid instead by Rohan who, with bloodshot eyes and a nervous, hunted look about him, seemed to be in even direr need. Rohan took one look at the bottle of rum, another at Aditya, and promptly bared his soul. He hadn't slept in three days, he said. The thought of marriage was suffocating him. And as luck would have it, during his journey to Lonavala, he had been accompanied by married people who weren't very good advertisements for matrimony.

Two aunts had hit on him. Three uncles had bitterly advised him against hitching up. And six kids, the inevitable early outcome of most Indian marriages, had not particularly endeared themselves to him. 'Why are most husbands and wives so mean to each other, so vindictive?' Rohan wanted to know from Aditya. 'How can they hate each other so much after just a few years of marriage?' He begged Aditya for advice.

It is never a good idea to seek advice from a sexed-up bachelor in the midst of a particularly prolonged dry spell. Aditya weighed in heavily against marriage. Rohan tried to put up a fight but was convinced within two minutes. He shared details of how he had agreed to the marriage with Aaliya in a moment of post-orgasmic weakness. With the bottle of rum at the halfway mark, the conversation steered around to how Rohan was to break up with Aaliya. And the most important question: whom should Rohan tell first, Aaliya or his parents? Aditya voted for Aaliya while Rohan chose his parents. But after they had considered the risk of potential violence on Aaliya's part, Aditya changed his mind.

Aditya walked away from Rohan in the mellow haze of a good deed done. He rounded a corner and came face to face with Leena. Leena was an ex-girlfriend with whom he had had a serious affair; even their respective parents had met. Leena—great in bed, neurotic, forever angry, and an ambitious career woman of the type who ate nails and balls for breakfast—had never forgiven him for breaking up with her. What was Leena doing here at the wedding? Especially on this remote resort where he had no chance of escape.

Leena was strangely sweet, though. It turned out that she once gone to college with Aaliya. In Aditya's book, that was strike two for Aaliya. It was a good thing that Rohan was breaking up with her. Leena mentioned that he was still looking good, despite the few pounds he had put on. No one could give a back-handed compliment quite like her, Aditya knew. She ran a finger lightly over his face and walked on, leaving him mystified. It had been exactly 2,032 days since he had last received a compliment from her, back-handed or otherwise. And the feather-light touch had made him giddy, and reminded him of what else could follow.

At the appointed time, the bar was thrown open. As Aditya threw on his jacket, he thought about inviting the room-mate along, but he took one look at him poring over *The Wall Street Journal* on his iPad and decided that he was already in a happy place. On his way to the bar, he bumped into Urvi. Finally! He smiled his broadest smile. She hers. Things finally seemed to be looking up. That was when she dropped the dreaded 'B' word and called him bhaiyya. From long, painful experience, Aditya knows that this was a barrier which couldn't be overcome. Urvi then proceeded to ply him with numerous questions. On business. The economy. Politics. Global warming. Obama. Osama. Sheikh Makhtoom el Burj Al Khalifa. Okay, not the last one. She looked at him with sincere, earnest eyes. I can learn so much from you, she said.

After she had asked for the nth time what was wrong with him, he excused himself and stumbled to the bar where he met Sabah. She looked around quickly, saw that no one was watching, grabbed his arm and dragged him behind a phone booth. She kissed him hungrily. Afterwards, she said how much she had wanted to do so ever since she had reconnected with him. She then walked away.

Aditya ordered himself an extra-large rum and coke. He

then got one of the younger brats to take Urvi's glass to her, with the incentive that he could sip from it on the way. He was just halfway through his drink when Sabah walked up to the bar for a refill, her eldest in tow. He sent her kid over with another drink for Urvi, even though she had barely begun on her earlier one. Sabah grabbed him again and dragged him to the same corner as soon her kid's back was turned. 'Thanks,' she muttered, in the midst of steamy kisses and wild groping. She then walked away again. Infidelity, another great reason for Rohan not to be getting married, Aditya mused, slowly sipping his drink. Sabah was hot, he thought. There was something about these married babes, probably the years of repression.

Aaliya and her mates arrived, upping the glamour quotient of the crowd by a couple of degrees. Meghna and Leena hit the hitherto uninhabited dance floor and did their thing. Their swaying hemlines, the mesmerizing cleavages and steamy moves ensured that all eyes remained fixed on the floor. As he saw Sabah walk towards the bar, slightly unsteady, his future plan of action became clear to Aditya. He introduced his nerdy room-mate to Urvi and impressed on her how knowledgeable the banker was. He also told her that he had a degree from IIM-A which, for some reason, all chicks seem to dig. He made it clear to his room-mate how imperative it was for him to not return to the room for the next hour. He then quietly took Sabah to his room while all eyes were still glued to the dance floor.

The sex was brief, intense and liberating for both. When Sabah orgasmed, she did so with the violence and intensity of a tightly coiled spring being released. She took her time with her second coming, and stretched it out for as long as she could, memorizing it with every muscle of her body. Afterwards, they lay naked for a bit. She lay on her side, one leg thrown over his body, her head in the crook of his shoulder, and idly fondled his cock and balls, re-familiarizing herself with the contours of the male organ. He ran his hand down her smooth back, dipped into the small of it, and admired the rounded firmness of her perfect ass. She murmured that Rohan and Aaliya made a lovely couple. He mentioned, as casually as possible, that they might not be together for long. She didn't seem unduly worked up by the prospect. Thinking they might be missed if they remained away for too long, Sabah and Aditya rose, dressed, kissed, and went out.

The dance floor had been taken over by the Punjabis and resembled the streets of New York during the Occupy Wall Street movement. Each of Aaliya's friends had at least seven bhangra blokes bouncing around her. They jerked around uncontrollably, eyes fixed firmly on the bosoms heaving before them. The initial josh had all but vanished, and had been replaced by whiskey-fuelled testosterone.

Rohan appeared midway through it all. He whispered that he was still undecided. His nerve had given way on seeing his parents dancing in obvious joy. His current POA was to divorce Aaliya after one year of marriage. To assuage his parents' feelings, he would tell them that she didn't want children, or some such thing. There was nothing Aditya could think of to sort out Rohan's confusion so he kept quiet. A heavy mist had settled over the party and through a gap in the swirls, he could catch occasional glimpses of Urvi sitting on an isolated bench with his room-mate, deep in conversation. So, two good things happened today, he mused. Just then, he caught sight of Sabah skulking in the shadows near his room, having put her husband and her kids to bed. Make that three, he thought as he walked to his room.

Their lovemaking the second time around was slower and more languorous, even though it lacked the earlier animal frenzy. Sabah was eager to give him pleasure in every way even as she made sure that he paid her back in full. When she rode him, she was even coy, and asked him if the Caesarian scar on her lower abdomen put him off. But he assured her that it in no way lessened the beauty of her perfect body. And he sincerely meant it. As he gazed up at her rocking back and forth, intent on taking him into her as deep as she could, he wondered if it was motherhood which gave her those gorgeous breasts, and the patience to cater to every whim of his. When his roommate cousin knocked on the door, Aditya—bare except for a towel wrapped around him—stuck his head outside the door and gave the banker a short lecture on the health benefits of long, late-night walks. Before he could say anything, Rohan shut the door on his face.

Sabah told him about her husband's boring sexual habits and about the lack of adventure and romance in her life. If he was Hrithik Roshan, she said to Aditya by way of example, her husband was Saurabh Shukla. She then abruptly stood up and left, admitting that it would be very difficult to leave if she stayed any longer.

Aditya, now relaxed and no longer sex-crazed, turned to conquest number two as he finally allowed his shivering roomie to re-enter the room.

His sleep was rudely interrupted at around 10 a.m. by the shrill ringing of the phone in the room. It was his mother. She was agitated and yelling at him. She wanted to know where he had disappeared the previous night. And most importantly, what had he said about the wedding being called off? He did the honourable thing and flatly denied having said anything of the sort. He promised to meet her for breakfast. His mother pointed out that the breakfast had been cleared off half an hour earlier. His doorbell began to ring furiously. The person ringing the bell was also simultaneously banging on the door. His room-mate, who must have been used to a more sedate life, was standing on his bed in fear, covering himself with his bed-sheet. Aditya promised his mom that he would be with her in five minutes. He then opened the door to let Aaliya in.

'What the fuck was that about my wedding being called off, you bhenchod?' she said without preamble. As she entered the room, she gave the roomie such a murderous look that he scampered off, not even bothering to wear his night suit. Aditya's musings on how sexy he found women who use Hindi gaalis were drowned by the choice abuse which rolled freely off Aaliya's tongue. After she had cooled off a bit, she confessed that she knew Rohan was having second thoughts about their marriage. What she wanted to know was what he had actually said to Aditya. The phone rang. It was Rohan's mom. She told Aditya that Rohan was missing. She also wanted to know what was with the news about the wedding being called off. He promised to be with her in five minutes and hung up. He then gave Aaliya a gist of the conversation with her to-be or not-to-be future mother-in-law. He also gave her an even briefer gist of his talk with Rohan, skipping over the incriminating bits and his advice. He then added, not very convincingly, that Rohan appeared to have changed his mind when he had last met him at the bar. Again, he skipped over Rohan's plan to divorce her.

Aaliya, the perfectly proportioned Amazon, was on the verge of tears. Which was a very unusual thing. She soon started to sob. Aditya knew better than to try to comfort her. He just stood beside her with a glass of water in hand, muttering, 'There, there.' Her fury returned as soon as she drank water. She came straight to the point. She needed his support, she said. She needed him to convince Rohan. Sarcastically, she added that he was Rohan's trusted friend and adviser, which was a pity. He had just begun to mumble his protest when she interrupted him with an offer. If he promised to convince Rohan, she said that she would ensure that Meghna slept with him. He mumbled some more, about how that wasn't necessary, and what did she take him for, when she raised the stakes and the temperature of the room. She promised him that if Rohan went through with the marriage—'It will be in the confused, commitment-phobic asshole's best interest to do so!'—she would ensure that Meghna participated in a threesome with him. Aditya stopped mumbling. He promised her on all that was holy to him that her marriage would take place as planned. He then asked her the obvious question. Meghna owed her a threesome, was Aaliya's simple reply. Before he could ask anything else, someone came up to the door.

Aaliya, on being told that it was probably his or Rohan's mom, escaped nimbly over the rear balcony. As she left, she asked, 'So, do we have a deal?' With visuals of a naked Meghna in his head, he ambled to the door which was now shuddering under the onslaught.

It was Rohan, who had a dreamy expression on his face. Aditya knew from years of torture that the expression was usually the precursor to a lot of pain. For him. Rohan seemed completely oblivious to the events of the morning. He was dressed in his track-suit and sneakers and was in a strangely romantic mood. He commented on the weather. The lush green colours of the surrounding hills. The lovely mist which kept rolling in and out. He even had a few nice words for Lady Gaga.

Aditya interrupted his reverie by recycling some of Aaliya's best expletives.

'Don't worry,' Rohan announced grandly, 'I've decided to get married after all.' This was going to be easy, thought a relieved Aditya, naked Meghna popping up in his head once more.

'But to Leena,' added Rohan, smiling nervously.

She was the one for him, didn't Aditya see that? The fact that he'd hated her, and couldn't stand her when she and Aditya were dating, was brushed aside and attributed to his immaturity at the time. 'But she's a psycho,' Aditya said. 'She's a goddess!' was Rohan's soft, puppy-like reply. The phone rang yet again, interrupting their conversation. It was his mom who, with sarcasm and anger dripping from her voice, wanted to know when his five minutes would come to an end. He hung up with a deep sense of foreboding. The naked Meghna was fully clad now, and blowing a raspberry at him. A lot hinged on what he said next. He decided to begin gently. Don't be a gaandu motherfucker, he began, and was about to continue in the same vein when the phone rang again. It was Rohan's mom, who had the same questions as his mother had had. After quickly reassuring her, he brought Rohan up to speed with Sabah's indiscretion and the rumours about the wedding. He excluded Aaliya's visit entirely but felt it appropriate to mention that she was prowling around with a machete, looking for his head to mount on a wall.

Rohan now came clean. He had met Leena early in the morning, he said, just as he was setting off for a walk in the mist. She had offered to come along. She had listened to him patiently, and had intently heard every word of whatever he had to say. This never happened with Aaliya. They had enjoyed the magical, misty sunrise together. Oh yes, they had kissed. Many times, too. Aditya stepped in then, and asked if Rohan had told Leena about how he was beginning to feel about Aaliya and their impending marriage. If he hadn't, everything would be fine; it could be put down to temporary insanity caused by the shock of being exposed to sunrise. Rohan denied saying anything to Leena, but wouldn't meet Aditya's eyes.

They then began doing what any two reasonable males would under the circumstances. They began listing out the pros and the cons of the two women: Aaliya and Leena. It didn't take much time for the verdict to swing completely in favour of Aaliya. Rohan made a sneaky effort, trying to give Long Term Happiness, which he had listed as a pro for Leena, additional weightage. But Aditya was well prepared for such a manoeuvre. He promptly gave the same weightage to Parents' Happiness which had been listed as a pro for Aaliya. His move took the wind out of Rohan's sails

Someone was at the door again. Rohan complained about being interrupted but when he was told that one or both of their mothers were probably at the door, he sneaked out over the balcony. Before leaving, he promised Aditya that he would not contact Leena till they met again.

Both the mothers were at the door and were angry at having been kept waiting. Aditya blamed the delay on loose motions, an excuse he had successfully used to get himself out of many a troublesome situation. He assured both that the situation was under control. Rohan was nervous, that was all, and needed love and sympathy. He could also use a hard warning, he said, looking at Rohan's mom, that he had to go through with the wedding. Velvet glove, steel fist. Or soft smile, iron teeth. Something like that. Both the mothers liked what they were hearing. His mom instantly became solicitous about his health, which was a great sign. She wanted to know about the quantity, the frequency, the colour and the viscosity of his motions. Which wasn't a good sign and usually a precursor to awful-tasting home remedies and a complete ban on alcohol. He assured her that he was well and recovering. When the banging on the door began again, he automatically pointed to the balcony before he realized the mistake he was making. All three of them went to the door but found no one there. Which was curious. Rohan's mom thanked him and promised that she would do exactly as he had said. As his mom left, she made him promise to do exactly as she said. He was to take a mixture of jeera, gur and neem ka pani; it was the foolproof cure for his loose motions.

He shut the door and turned around, mentally undressing Meghna, only to find Sabah removing her bra. She had entered his room via the balcony. Her husband was apparently snoring again, after a particularly heavy breakfast. The kids were swimming. He wanted to ask her about her indiscretion, but the sight of a topless woman has changed many a man's priorities. At that precise moment, there was a knock on the door. 'Ya Allah!' Sabah exclaimed as she held up her top to cover her chest.

It was the roomie, shivering. Aditya handed him his track top and replicated the look Aaliya had given him earlier. It had the same impact. He disappeared. These IIM-A types, he thought, nothing prepares them for real life. He then returned to his third session of love-making.

By mutual consensus, they both rated the third time as the best. For him the warmth of her embrace and their naked tenderness contrasted well with the madness of the morning. For her, as she shyly confessed after, there was something delightful about making love in the daylight. She always felt like a criminal, she said, when sex happened at night. Or under the covers. Here, in the broad daylight, with the breeze blowing from the balcony, with someone loving her for a change instead of just fucking her like an animal, it was perfect. She felt free, liberated. Her words touched a chord in him. They made him do something he rarely did. He went down on her. He used his tongue below and ran his hands over her thighs, breasts and pussy. She came multiple times. It was her first experience of being eaten out. Cunnilingus wasn't in her Saurabh Shukla's repertoire. Afterwards, he gently dressed her up. Just as they were sharing a tender moment, someone arrived at the door. She exited quietly from the balcony, blowing a kiss at him as she did so. Aditya mentally filed a note to write 'build a staircase in balcony' in the resort feedback form.

He opened the door to find the room-mate and Urvi outside, the former shivering, the latter looking cross. Aditya smiled at him, looked at his watch and told them that they could have the room for an hour. And before either of them could react, he exited from the balcony, making his way to his friend's room.

Rohan was relieved to see him. His mom had just given him an earful, he said. And his dad had threatened to disown him. Aaliya had promised him with varieties of torture which even the CIA did not currently sanction. Leena had paid him a visit as well, but Rohan, adhering strictly to instructions, had pretended to be out. He now sat with his head in his hands, wondering who was going to come and threaten him next. They talked it over, calmly, man to man and went through all the logic again. Everything was all still heavily in favour of him going through with the marriage to Aaliya. Rohan's mouth voiced the words but his eyes were blank. He checked dully with Aditya to see if he had destroyed the list of pros and cons they had made in his room. When Aditya said no, Rohan began to curse him. After the twelfth gaali, Aditya called a stop to Rohan's rant and promised to do something about it immediately. He also volunteered to talk to Leena and figure out how the land lay, so to speak. Rohan hugged him before he left.

As luck would have it, he spotted Leena standing with Meghna next to the swimming pool. As he approached, they turned and looked at him. Leena whispered something in Meghna's ear and they both began to giggle. Unfazed, he walked up to them and asked Leena if he could have a word with her in private, flashing his best smile at Meghna, determined to leave a good impression on her.

'What are you up to?' he asked Leena as soon as they were by themselves. She ignored his questions and ran her fingers over his face and the exposed part of his chest, giving him goosebumps all over. 'Not now, Leena,' he said sternly. 'Why are you trying to ruin Rohan's life? And isn't Aaliya your childhood friend?' She stopped feeling him up.

'He told you?' she asked.

Rohan took another crack at her. 'Look, you know he is vulnerable and nervous right now. Please don't confuse him anymore. You have to back off, surely you realize that. Else no one is going to be happy anymore.'

They realized they were attracting too much attention in public so he invited her to his room, entering from the balcony just because it was closer. They ended up interrupting a groping, kissing, fumbling session between his roomie and Urvi. The guilty pair was scandalized and quickly left the room; Urvi gave him a dirty glance as she left. He sat opposite Leena and began to calmly talk to her. She heard him patiently, but her fingers began doing their stuff again, moving in tiny circles. After a few minutes, she leaned forward and kissed him. He tried to talk some more but she kissed him again, her fingers now picking up the tempo. 'I am so lonely,' she cried. 'Rohan has you for a friend. I have no one.' Aditya promptly stopped speaking about Rohan and began to kiss her back.

Her fingers, finding the privacy of the room encouraging, caressed his chest for a few moments, jumped over his belly, and began describing small circles on the inside of his thigh which progressively gained in circumference. The first time her fingertip caressed his crotch, Aditya twitched. She leaned forward to kiss him. He tried to disengage and conclude their discussion, but the tongue which was tickling his tonsils prevented him from speaking.

He was pleased to find that he could get so hard, so quickly, given his recent exertions with Sabah—he still had it! When she slipped off her clothes, he could see that she had become a fuller, curvier woman. Leena was in no mood for foreplay. She helped him out of his shirt and his trousers and led him by the hand to the bed. She lay down, pulling him on top of her. She helped him out of his briefs and guided him inside. To his surprise, he found that flesh remembered flesh, and they settled into a frantic, familiar rhythm. But the bed was creaky and kept banging against the wall. Bearing in mind the flimsiness of the partitions in the resort, Aditya briefly stopped to reach across and switch on the TV and find the FTV channel. He turned the volume way up and then quickened his pace and force. She then made a move which they once practiced very often, but which had now slipped his mind. The moment she did it, though, it all came flooding back. Just as he had begun the final ascent to his climax, she paused, pushed him on to his side, quickly slid out from under and straddled him. She reached down, had him wrap his arms around her lower back, and clutching the back of his head, smothered his face between her breasts. Ah, still the control freak, Aditya thought. He let her have her way, and allowed her to dictate the pace of her climax. She rocked with increasing violence until she came to a shuddering orgasm. Quickly, she slipped off him and expertly masturbated him until he went over the edge. After he had spurted all over the bed, she dressed, saying playfully, 'For this, I could stay out of Rohan's life forever.' She left the room via the balcony. And he lay back, utterly spent. It wasn't even lunch time yet.

Lunch was a quiet affair. Aditya reassured both his mom and Rohan's mom that all seemed settled. Rohan used the right words as well, and showed what seemed to be genuine enough contrition. Sabah was busy with her brood but winked at him a couple of times. Urvi and his IIM-A roomie seemed inseparable. Love, peace and harmony were in the air. But it all rapidly changed when Leena barged in, her eyes blazing and her hair dishevelled.

Aaliya and Meghna followed a step behind. Leena picked up a fork, walked up threateningly to Aditya and, with her volume just loud enough for everyone in the resort to hear her words, said, 'You bastard! Did you do this only for a threesome! You're disgusting!' Aaliya made apologetic sounds and gestures from behind Leena but Aditya instinctively knew that this, despite his reputation, would take some living down. As calmly as he could, and keeping the moms at bay, he shepherded the three women to his room. Rohan followed all of them into Aditya's room. His curiosity was piqued.

The door to his room had barely shut when Leena commanded Rohan to disregard all the advice he had ever got from Aditya. He was only doing it because Aaliya had promised him a threesome with Meghna.

'The threesome wasn't supposed to include me,' Aaliya anxiously clarified.

Rohan looked at both Aaliya and Aditya with wounded eyes.

Aditya hastened to assure Rohan. 'But, everything I told you is true,' he said.

'This promise, was it made last night or today?' was Rohan's only question.

'The promise was made today morning,' revealed Leena damagingly.

'Did you know Leena went for an early morning walk with Rohan and they kissed?' Aditya announced, deciding that attack was the best form of defence.

There were loud gasps from Aaliya and Meghna and a small one from Leena, who was surprised at having been betrayed, especially in light of their pre-lunch work-out.

'Meghna told me she was available in case things didn't turn out well between you and me,' Rohan yelled, determined to deflect attention off of himself.

'When?' hissed Aaliya, glaring at Meghna.

'Some time ago,' came Rohan's weak, stammering reply.

'Well, if we're discussing the past, Aaliya once took part in a threesome at my behest,' said a spirited Meghna, determined not to be the guilty one.

Turning to Rohan, Aaliya said, 'That was before you.'

'He slept with me, today!' yelled Leena, pointing an accusing finger at Aditya, equally determined to be the centre of attention. The knocking which sounded on the door mercifully prevented people from saying more incriminating things.

It was Urvi. 'Bhaiyya, what is this list about?' she asked Aditya as she marched into the room, waving their list of pros and cons of the morning. Aditya reacted first. He swiftly plucked the paper from Urvi's hand, crumpled it, and put it into his mouth. He rolled it around for a while before noisily swallowing it. 'It is an old habit,' Rohan said unconvincingly. 'When he's stressed, he eats paper.'

Aditya decided it was time to take charge. He escorted Urvi out of the door and shut the door behind her despite her protests. 'Look,' he said firmly, 'Rohan was confused and that is the truth. Despite any promises made to me, I truly believe the choice he's made, to get married to Aaliya, is the right one.'

He then looked at Leena, 'I also truly believe that he fell for you only because he was so vulnerable and confused. It wouldn't have lasted. He used to hate you when we were going around and used to call you psycho.' Leena grimaced but nodded her head in agreement.

Aditya continued, 'Aaliya did promise me a threesome in the morning, but you have to trust me, it doesn't change anything I told you.'

Something clicked inside Rohan and he held out his hand for a high five with Aditya.

'What's this?' Meghna asked as she sat on Aditya's bed, pulling out a pink, lacy bra from under her shapely bottom. A small box of chocolates lay next to the bra, along with a note which said 'Something to remember me by'.

It was Sabah's writing, which only Rohan and Aditya recognized. 'You fucker,' Rohan said, 'is no female safe from you?'

'Focus, focus,' hissed Aditya, 'not now.' When someone arrived and started banging at the door again.

It was Aditya's mom who nervously peeked in, almost as if she expected blood to be spattered all over the room. Rohan's mom, just a foot behind, was doing the same. She enquired if everyone was okay. Aditya and Rohan gave her an affirmative response, followed a few seconds later by Aaliya. Both the mothers' faces lit up with joy and relief

'Why don't you also get married now?' pleaded Aditya's mom. 'Look Leena is here, too. I've never understood why the two of you broke up. You look so lovely together.'

Rohan decided to become a turncoat. 'Yes, that is a brilliant idea,' he said, enjoying the stricken look which came over Aditya's face. 'Let's make it a double wedding. In fact, I refuse to get married unless Aditya gets hitched as well.'

Aaliya's voice rang out sharply. 'You will do no such thing!' She then looked at her mom-in-law and said, 'Aunty, we still have a lot to sort out amongst us. Rohan and I will get married first, the others can decide for themselves what they want to do.'

Both moms nodded reluctantly at the sense she made. Aditya heaved a sigh of relief. The mothers decided to go, leaving the young ones to carry on. At the door, though, Aditya's mom turned back, and with the brazenness and insensitivity typical of mothers, enquired about his motions and if they were better now.

Epilogue

- Sabah couldn't hook up with Aditya again. Her Saurabh Shukla apparently suspected something and she didn't want to take a risk.
- The banker room-mate, egged on by Urvi, finally grew a spine and politely told Aditya to take a hike. Aditya used the opportunity to recover his health with long, freezing walks in the mist.
- Leena and Aditya, understandably, stayed out of each other's way for the rest of the weekend.
- In the bus which took them to the bottom of the hill after the wedding, Aditya found himself sandwiched between his mom and Rohan's mother. He had a faint premonition of disaster.
- Shortly after the wedding, Aditya—despite the wedding which had affirmed that he still had it—gave in to parental pressure and registered with a popular matrimonial site. Once he had filled out his profile and checked all the boxes in his preferences, he clicked 'Search for Partner'. The first profile which the website returned was that of Leena's. Fate, as they say, isn't without a sense of humour.

■

A Boat-Party on the Hooghly

In Room 502 of the Tollygunje Club, Dipesh was using his fingers to pleasure Amolika, making her moan and writhe in fevered excitement. He alternated between using one finger and two while he hungrily slurped her breasts. This carried on for a few more minutes, then Amolika paused her leg-thrashing and her ecstatic groans, turned to Dipesh, and asked in her lovely, Bengali-accented English, 'Are two fingers going to be enough, you think?'

Just then, a soulful jazz number began to play. It was Dipesh's ringtone. Both froze. They knew exactly who was calling. Amolika, never one to mince her words, said, 'If we were married and you had some senti crap like that as a ringtone for me, I'd never speak to you again!'

Then her phone began playing a mournful Rabindra Sangeet recital about walking alone. It was now Dipesh's turn. 'If we were married, and you had that as your ringtone, I would have to divorce you.'

Amolika laughed her deep-throated laugh and said dismissively, 'I don't know why I bother. Amrish is a Jat, he hardly gets it.'

And with that, after both had ignored the calls from their respective spouses, they returned to Dipesh's three fingers and his tongue.

Amolika had been married to Amrish for two years but had known and loved Dipesh for ten. Dipesh was married to Drishti, but had eyes only for Amolika. At first, the couples had got along well, they had even holidayed together, but now, especially with Dipesh and Amolika getting a little too carried away, they could barely stand each other. All four confided in their common friend, Shantanu, who was married to Shomili. Unlike his friends, Shantanu's marriage was happy.

Amolika's school friend, Piyali, was set to join this group of cross-connected friends. She was to be married to classmate Prasenjit, scion of one of the largest business houses in Kolkata. But Piyali was besotted with Mihir, another classmate and her childhood sweetheart.

All of these people were to come together for one night on a barge on the Hooghly River, at the engagement party thrown by Piyali's father.

■

Genial, plump Shantanu wiped his forehead as he walked up the gangway on to the barge. It wasn't just Kolkata's unendurable humidity—or the thought of being on this barge for three hours as it made a leisurely trip to the Dakshineswar Kali Temple and back—that was making him sweat. He didn't have a good feeling at all about tonight. It seemed like matters were about to come to a head; there was tension in the air.

And most importantly, he really wished people would stop confiding in him. Apart from Amolika, Dipesh and their respective spouses, all of whom separately confided in him, there was the bride-to-be, Piyali, and her childhood sweetheart, Mihir, who also poured their hearts out to him. Yes, he had known all of them for many years. Yes, he was a discreet, trustworthy man. Yes, he was happily married and did not run around chasing saris, and thus projected a solid, steadfast image. And, of course, he was a big shot, one of the seniormost IAS officers of Kolkata.

But he had a high-stress job with long working hours and a high-maintenance wife; this mess was the last thing he needed.

Amolika, walking just a few steps ahead of Shantanu, was lost in thought, too. Memories of the furious lovemaking at the Tolly Club still washed over her. Last night had been Amolika and Dipesh's tenth 'anniversary'. Given the occasion, they had both, quite recklessly, decided to meet, and to make love. Dipesh's skill with his fingers and tongue weren't his only accomplishments. And that they had met after a long time only increased the intensity of the encounter. In fact, she had had her first orgasm when he had taken off his shirt and she had run her hands over his familiar, taut, muscular body.

She was jerked abruptly back to the present when Amrish tried to hold her hand. She brushed it aside. Amrish said, scowling, 'I just wanted to know if you're okay. You didn't respond even after I called out to you thrice.'

Drishti—who was walking with Dipesh a few steps behind Amolika and Amrish, and in front of Shantanu—said in a deliberately shrill voice, 'Dipesh, if you so much as say "Hi" to Amolika, or even stand near her tonight, I will walk out of this marriage!'

Shantanu could see Amrish stiffen. Amolika turned back, glaring malevolently.

Greeting her guests, Piyali had such a distracted air that almost everyone commented, 'Nervous, huh?' 'You okay, babe?' Her hug with Amolika, her school friend, and Shantanu, her confidante, lingered a fraction longer than that with the others. 'We need to talk,' was the common message for both.

The loud boat-horn rent the air, startling some into spilling their drinks. With an almighty shudder and heave, accompanied by a loud phut-phut-phut of the diesel engine, the boat began its journey on the vast, silent river.

Piyali quietly walked up to Shantanu and touched his arm just as he put the first, satisfying whisky-soda of the evening to his lips. (Thanks to the fact that she was marrying into wealth, Piyali's dad had forsaken his usual Blender's Pride and was serving Chivas Regal.)

'Shantanu,' she said, when they were relatively alone. 'I met Mihir again yesterday night. We made love. Is that bad?'

Shantanu had very little room to manoeuvre. So he simply grunted, patted her on the back and walked away. Piyali, meanwhile, sat at the head of the boat, on one of the benches which lined the deck, sipping her Absolut-and-Coke, watching the placid waters of the Hooghly flow by, reminiscing about the previous night.

She didn't know it, but their tryst, like Amolika and Dipesh's, had been arranged by Shantanu—it was through his good offices that a room at the Club had been made available. Amolika and Dipesh had used it in the afternoon, and they had done so in the night.

Mihir had fucked her with the desperate frenzy of a man who knew that it was unlikely that he would be able to do so again in the near future. She had been in a more sentimental, let's-talk, kind of mood but, on sensing his urgency, had immersed herself in the moment without a second thought. He'd bitten her a couple of times, determined to leave his mark. At the moment, she hadn't cared. All she had been capable of doing was to feel his heft on top of her, breathe in and breathe out as his arms tightened and loosened around her, and hear his husky voice whisper into her ears. He pumped her vigorously, kneading flesh with both hands: her breasts, buttocks, anything that he could find. He reached behind to lift her by her hip, reaching as deep as he could into her. He wanted her flesh to remember his.

Piyali had known Mihir for ten years, through much of which they had dated in secret, out of fear of Piyali's authoritarian dad. Things had looked up briefly when Mihir had joined Citibank in a sales position. Piyali's father, who was used to seeing Mihir hovering around his daughter, had briefly thought that Mihir had finally realized the importance of material success. (In his opinion, Mihir was an intelligent but grossly misguided young man.) But within a couple of years, Mihir had left Citi, hating the culture, his life, his job, his prospects and, instead, had set up a musical band and become its lead singer. Dad had minced no words in expressing his disgust to Piyali and her mom at Mihir's decision, 'Pagal ladka. Sirf gaane se pet thodi bharta hai. Bewakuf, pachtayega,' and had coolly, without a second thought, crossed him off his list of potential grooms for his precious daughter. When another schoolmate, Prasenjit, the quiet, humble, hard-working son of one of the richest men in Kolkata, had come, by himself and without any ceremony, to seek Piyali's hand in marriage, almost as soon as Mihir had left for Mumbai to carve out his singing future there, Piyali's father had been beside himself with delight. And Piyali had found it very difficult to put up a fight against the perfect logic with which her father had recommended Prasenjit.

Prasenjit's family, too, despite initial reservations about the two families' unequal social status, had been won over by Piyali's stunning looks and their son's stubbornness.

Piyali drained her drink, watched the boat cross Prinsep Ghat and looked down at her chest; a bite mark was visible just above her bra, barely covered up by the low-cut blouse she was wearing underneath her diaphanous sari. Looking at the mark aroused her as she sat by herself, toying with the empty glass.

■

Amolika's case was complicated. She and Dipesh had been inseparable friends for many years but had never dated. Though they shared the same interests—soccer, squash and sex, as a witty friend had pointed out—they had actually set each other up with different partners for many years. And then, three years ago, they had inexplicably, suddenly and irrevocably fallen for each other.

Out of respect for her ailing, old-fashioned father, who was against the 'newfangled' love marriage, she had never revealed that Dipesh was anything but a good friend. And then one day, the family doctor took her aside. He told her that, as per the latest tests, her father, a long-suffering heart patient, was now terminal. He needed to be pampered, humoured and looked after. And he was to be given no shock whatsoever.

Her father had then asked her to fulfill a single request of his. She was to marry a man of his choice while he was still alive. His business partner's son, Amrish. That way he could die assured that his daughter's well-being would be taken care of. How could she refuse the man who, ever since her mother's death, had been everything to her, who had never refused her anything?

Amrish and she were married within a month, after many tearful meetings with Dipesh. Her friends, including Shantanu, begged her to speak to her father, who had been a reasonable man when well. But it was as if a cloud of filial duty had descended upon her. She went with the flow. Over time she found plenty to like in the solid, dependable Amrish, whom she had known since childhood but had never given a second glance. The cloud, though, dissipated almost immediately on her father's death a few months after their marriage. Her intense longing for her soulmate, Dipesh, returned who, in the meantime, had given in to his family's demands and had married Drishti. But now, it was almost as if the two, separated for almost a year, were hell-bent on making up for lost time, regardless of the consequences.

Shantanu winced when Amolika sat next to him, two gin-and-tonics down, despite their barely having reached Eden Gardens. 'Yesterday was special, intense, magical. What am I doing, Shantanu?' she asked.

He shook his head mournfully. And saying, 'I have no idea, Amolika,' he touched her affectionately on the head.

'The sex was so good, that I think I'm still trembling. We…'

she couldn't complete her sentence because Shantanu, with a terse, 'Spare me the details,' made his way to the bar for a refill.

'Thanks for the room yesterday, bro,' said Dipesh, quietly coming up alongside, getting himself a drink.

'Tu kya kar raha hai, Dipesh?' Shantanu asked exasperatedly.

Dipesh shook his head. 'I've told Amolika, let's divorce our spouses and get married. She's a bit confused right now. She feels she owes Amrish for having taken care of the business after Baba's death, and the fair way he has given her family their share. But I agree with you, we can't go on like this.'

'I told both her and you this before she got married. "You both love each other. Speak to Baba or have your parents speak to him." You developed cold feet then. Now what is done is done. Think of how much unhappiness you will cause…' He shut up as someone came up to the bar, took his drink and walked off. He was glad that at least Mihir hadn't been invited to the party. What was the best advice he could give Dipesh or Amolika, he wondered?

Amrish then walked up to stand beside him, carrying a whisky in one hand and Amolika's gin-and-tonic in the other—she was dancing on the packed floor. 'Have you seen the way Dipesh is always hovering around Amolika?' he asked, the familiar scowl playing on his face. 'Just can't stay away from her, the bastard!'

Shantanu chose not to respond. He had known Amrish since their schooldays. Nothing much had changed in Amrish's behaviour since then. If he couldn't fix a problem, he would either abuse or get into a fist fight. He was just raring to brawl with Dipesh, Shantanu could see, and that was a dangerous sign. He tried to change the topic. 'How's business these days?' he asked.

'Just look at him, Shantanu,' Amrish said moodily, observing Dipesh chatting with Piyali. 'Have you ever seen him speak to anyone other than a woman? The fucker!'

'Amrish, let it be. You're only making yourself angry and that never does you any good.'

'Whose side are you on, Shantanu? That bugger is all over my wife! Am I supposed to do nothing? Just stand here and watch?'

'Its just a phase, Amrish, it will pass.'

'Well, that "phase" is fucking my wife! I *know* he is.'

'Why don't you first speak to your wife, instead of him?' Shantanu regretted the words almost as soon as he said them. He shuddered to think of the directions such a conversation would take the couple. But he looked on in amazement as Amrish simmered down.

After a long pause, he said, 'I can't say anything to her. She's still fragile after Baba's death. I think she needs some more time.' He gulped down his drink and walked away, just as the sound of trumpets rent the air.

Shantanu looked around to see four men blowing ceremonial curved trumpets walk out of the main cabin on the barge. Prasenjit was in the middle and was being showered with rose petals by two women walking behind them. He looked ill at ease; this grand entrance was obviously not his idea. Shantanu cheered loudly, throwing in a couple of wolf whistles for good measure.

Piyali joined him, linking her arm with his. 'He's sweet, but I can't get married to him,' she said, looking at Prasenjit. 'What do you think?'

'Piyali, this is not the first time we've had this conversation. The time for debate is over. You can't keep changing your mind.

I don't know what is wrong with both you and Amolika. I think you both are secret sisters. You've spent too much time together in school. Now it's a question of your dad's reputation and his business as well, by the way. Prasenjit's parents can ruin him completely. You know they own half of Kolkata.'

'But it's my life! How can I get married to someone I don't love?'

Shantanu mincingly imitated Piyali, '"How can I get married to someone I don't love?" What were you doing when your dad rejected Mihir? What were you doing when he accepted Prasenjit and announced your engagement six months ago? The time to think, feel, act was then, not now, on the day of your engagement, just one day before your wedding!'

'But at that time I didn't know how I would feel with Prasenjit, I'd never really spent much time with him. How could I take a stand? Yesterday, when I was with Mihir, I felt complete. His touch, his warmth, I can make love to him again and again, I can…'

'Please spare me the details. But I will say one thing: you've not yet, to the best of my knowledge, been with Prasenjit. So how can you feel the same way about him as you do about someone you have? And he is a lovely guy, humble and hard-working. How can you not even give him a chance?'

Piyali's brow furrowed, as her natural combativeness struggled with the truth of what Shantanu had just said to her. She was deep in thought when she spotted Drishti walking towards them. She gave Shantanu an absentminded peck on the cheek and Drishti a polite smile before leaving.

'Shantanu, I'm at my wits' end. You have to help me. He's seeing her, I'm sure of it.' Drishti's voice trembled. She was from

Delhi and was unfamiliar with most of Dipesh's gang. She felt alien, even unwanted, by most of them. Her father had known Shantanu's and had introduced her to him around the time the nuptials with Dipesh were being finalized and she had somehow, very quickly, warmed to this genial man, confiding in him to a degree she never thought she could to someone whom she had known for such a short while.

'Drishti, I really don't know what to say to you.'

'They are meeting, aren't they? Tell me. You must know.'

'That's not the question you have to ask yourself. The question you have to ask is, "Do I love him? Do I really want to stay with him?"'

Drishti tossed her hair back and thought for a while before saying calmly, 'If I can have the same Dipesh I had at the beginning of our marriage, I will stay with him forever. That person was alone, despite having so many friends. He needed love. He wanted to please me. He was hungry for me. We used to make love…'

'Spare me the details, spare me the details! What is wrong with you women?'

'Dipesh is worth fighting for, is all that I'm saying. Amolika changed some time after her father's death. Before then, we had even gone on a holiday together to Santiniketan, and to Phuket. Everything was fine, I swear to you. But after her baba passed away, the way she looks at Dipesh has changed completely. She almost makes love to him with her eyes. I can see her staring at him. And I know that Amrish feels as angry as I do.'

'It's just a phase, Drishti,' Shantanu said weakly. 'This too shall pass.'

'I can't just sit by and watch this happen, Shantanu. I have my pride, too, you know? I sometimes feel that half the problem is with this city. I hate it! Everything here; the club, the roads, the restaurants are a memory of both of them together.'

'Oye ma'am, you're speaking about the city I love!' said Shantanu mock-angrily, but somewhere in his head a flashbulb had been lit.

'Anyways,' Drishti stepped up and gave him a quick peck on his cheek, 'I don't know what I would do without you. I would've committed suicide, I think.'

'Suicide karein tumhare dushman…' he said after her as she walked back slowly towards the bar.

■

Just as the boat reached the picturesque and well-lit Armenian cemetery and picked up pace, Piyali walked up to Prasenjit and embarrassed him by slipping an arm around his waist. 'Come, I want to talk,' was all she said as she pulled him away. His complexion turned a bright beetroot red as he mumbled apologies to the people he had been talking to.

'But where are we going?' he asked as she led him down the stairs below the main cabin to the cabins in the hold, past the filthy galley where the staff was casually lounging about. He felt uncomfortable with the glances he and Piyali were getting but she seemed least bothered. She knew that a room had been reserved to keep gifts in. It was just below the engine room, towards the bow. She sent off the attendant posted there and, swiftly pulling Prasenjit inside, shut the door and turned to her alarmed husband-to-be.

'But, eta ki? What…what are you doing?

She took his hands and placed them on her waist.

'But…' he began. This time, she silenced him with a firm kiss on his lips.

'We're getting married tomorrow, Piyali. Shouldn't we wait and…' She laced her arms around his neck and kissed him again, her tongue parting his lips, seeking his. Pressed up against his groin she could feel something stir, but she sensed his hesitation.

'Make love to me,' she commanded.

■

'Dada, what do you think I should do?' Dipesh asked earnestly, or as earnestly as anyone three drinks down can do so. 'Whatever you say, I will do.' They were at the bar. Shantanu could see Amrish trying to drag a reluctant Amolika to the dance floor. Prasenjit's mom was frantically instructing some of his cousins to look for her son and would-be daughter-in-law.

'Stay away from Amolika, fall in love with your lovely wife and live happily ever after.'

'I can't do that, you know…'

'Then be miserable for the rest of your lives and make everyone around you unhappy.'

'Dada, in fact I haven't told you something. My company is sending me to UK for a year. I've convinced Amolika to come with me. We both intend to file for divorce and go away. By the time we come back, tempers and feelings will have cooled down and everything will be okay. What do you think?'

Shantanu could see Amolika dancing like a wooden doll. In the meantime, the search party for Piyali and Prasenjit returned empty-handed.

'I think that's a very bad idea,' said Shantanu heavily, but another flashbulb lit in his mind.

■

Piyali took Prasenjit's hands and placed them inside her blouse, on her breasts. She slipped hers inside his sherwani and was surprised to find his abdomen ripplingly muscled. She ran her hands over his body and asked, 'You go to the gym often?'

He nodded shyly. 'What's this?' he asked, gesturing with his eyes to the love bite on her breast.

'Just an allergy.'

He was about to say something more when she put her hand over his mouth and slipped his under her bra. Then she removed her hand and kissed him again, this time pressing her body hard against him, her left leg separating his.

His reaction now surprised her for the second time that evening. He picked her up quite easily and, with one hand, swept the gifts off the bed and on to the floor. He placed her on the bed. He then held her hands together, over her head, keeping them in place with a tight grip while with the other, he first lifted her sari, petticoat et al, over her waist and then swiftly removed her panties. Before she could react, he was inside her. 'Ohhhhhhh…' A loud gasp escaped her. He was massive, and in spite of herself, she loved it.

■

Amolika, walking slightly unsteadily due to all the dancing and the drinking, now walked up. 'Shantanu, tell me what to do.

Seriously, I'm very confused right now.'

'Seriously? Stay away from Dipesh, fall in love with your unhappy, loving husband and live happily ever after.'

She moodily stared into her drink. 'Dipesh has asked me to leave Amrish and join him in London. He says by the time his year there ends, everyone here will have gotten over the divorce.'

Part of what made Shantanu such a great confidante was his ability to know when to keep quiet.

'Maybe it's for the best. I can't take this hiding, lying, cheating, a-room-in-Tolly anymore. I loved the sex, don't get me wrong, but I also felt like a whore.'

Shantanu still maintained a stoic silence.

'I miss Baba,' she said. 'Sometimes, I feel he is responsible for the mess I am in. At other times I feel he did everything for my own good and I'm just not able to see that. Amrish is a lovely guy. A Rajput Jat, but a lovely guy. Sometimes I feel he loves me more than Dipesh does. And while Dipesh and I are so similar in so many ways, same hobbies etc., with Amrish, given our opposite natures, it's more interesting, definitely more so for the long run.'

Both Shantanu and Amolika caught sight of Piyali's father steaming towards them, his nostrils flaring. It was a familiar sight for both.

'By the way, thanks for the room,' Amolika said and gave him a hurried peck on the cheek before beating a hasty retreat.

'Shantanu, have you seen Piyali? We can't find her anywhere and we need to do the ring ceremony at the right muhurat! This girl is always up to the wrong thing at the wrong time!'

■

Piyali watched Prasenjit move and thought, Wow! This guy's a machine! She was exploding with pleasure, her sari and petticoat were bunched up around her waist, her panties had been thrown aside and her very expensive blouse was pushed up to expose her breasts. Prasenjit slammed into her with the precision, force and regularity of a piston. Her hands were pinned down by his. She was loving being dominated, which was very unusual for her.

A tiny yelp escaped her when he suddenly released her arms and, with both his hands, lifted her butt up to pump harder and deeper. Full of surprises, aren't you, my husband-to-be? she thought. He lifted both her legs in the air and with the other still supporting her buttocks, entered the home stretch. Oh, she loved it!

And then, for the first time, she began to think about life with Prasenjit in his palatial house off Judges Court Road and compared it to the seedy one-bedroom flat Mihir had shown her photos of. She saw Prasenjit looking at her, his face flushed with joy and full of love. By the time he came, her mind was made up. She squeezed and stroked his penis, gave it a kiss and then made her way up, till she reached his lips which were softer than she had imagined them to be.

She was soon engulfed by another kiss. His hands lifted her up by her bottom and his tongue sought hers as eagerly as hers had searched for his. She knew now what she had to do.

They heard some shouting from outside and the sound of a smaller vessel chugging its way alongside theirs. Someone was calling out to their captain of the boat to slow down. They hurriedly dressed and made their way up to the deck where they were greeted by a strange sight.

Mihir was standing on the prow of the smaller launch which

was now almost alongside them. He was waving his hand like a film star to an adoring crowd. Prasenjit swore under his breath while her father loudly exclaimed, 'What is he doing here?' as Mihir clambered up the steps of a rope ladder thrown down for him. To everyone's surprise, Piyali moved forward as soon as Mihir reached the deck, grabbed him by the arm and led him inside one of the rooms on the deck, brushing aside everyone in their way. People could see the two argue through the glass windows. Both were very angry, Mihir more than Piyali. Soon though, he simmered down and Piyali became dominant. In time, Mihir's shoulders slumped, defeated.

Mihir emerged first, slammed the door shut, walked angrily back to his rope ladder and, without saying a word to anyone, slid down to his boat and told the crew to take off. All his plans of making a grand entry on the boat, impressing her father, and whisking Piyali away had been shredded to tatters by the suddenly remorseless and pragmatic Piyali, who seemed to have no recollection anymore of the previous night's lovemaking. He was having to slink off now, as quickly as he could, with his tail truly between his legs. The boatman and crew were just settling down to some tea but they took one look at Mihir's face and restarted the engine. In a few minutes, they were a distant speck, moving full steam in the opposite direction to the party boat.

Piyali emerged and walking up to Prasenjit, linked her arm through his. This time he didn't blush. 'We won't see him again,' she said, looking up at Prasenjit. If her mother-in-law and father-in-law weren't looking on she would probably have kissed him. Prasenjit though, completely out of character, leaned forward and kissed her. And the parents beamed in joy just as the boat auspiciously reached the Kali temple and began its lazy U-turn back

Shantanu had observed everything and it helped make up his mind on what he had to do next. It was a high-stakes gamble but it was the best he could think of at that moment. With firmness of purpose, he first spoke to Dipesh, then to Amolika. He told them his plan and got them both to agree, not without difficulty, and promise to abide by his conditions.

Half an hour later, with Howrah bridge in sight, most of the guests sitting on the floor, including a few who'd passed out, Piyali came up to Prasenjit, holding two glasses of champagne. She gave him a glass. 'Well done,' he told her, 'you did good.'

'Yes,' she laughed, 'I took your advice.'

'Which part, exactly, of my advice?' Shantanu asked delicately.

'Oh, I had sex with him. You were absolutely right. I was being unfair to him, it was like comparing eggs and watermelons.' Piyali was famous for her mixed metaphors. 'And he was great, just awesome in bed, it was...' she caught sight of Shantanu waving his arms frantically yet again. 'Yes, yes, I'll spare you the gory details, but it was fantastic advice.' They both sipped their champagne reflectively.

'And that's fantastic advice you've given to Amolika, too,' she continued, 'She just told me. I think it's a masterstroke. Cheers to that.'

'Cheers,' said Shantanu, clinking his glass with hers while she pecked his cheek.

■

Shantanu was on his way back from a conference in London and

Eighteen Plus

on the flight, thought back to that night at the boat party and his plan. He had made Dipesh agree to take up the job in the UK and to take Drishti along with him. He had made both Dipesh and Amolika promise to not contact each other for that entire one year period. And he, in turn, had promised them that if, after the year was over, they still wanted to leave their respective spouses and get together, he would find a way to hook them up. They had both agreed and a few days later, Dipesh had left, Drishti following soon after. As Shantanu had suspected, the one year had rapidly passed and they had stayed on in London, with Dipesh loving it there, doing very well, showing no signs of returning to India and Kolkata soon becoming a distant memory as they, together, explored the lovely, romantic cities of Europe. Back home, Amolika and Amrish were still always fighting but were deeply in love. And Prasenjit always let Piyali have her own way, or so he led her to believe, quietly getting his own way when important. Mihir was now was a big shot in Bollywood, but his music didn't so well in Kolkata. Perhaps Prasenjit's owning the largest music store chain of the city had something to do with it.

With a satisfied sigh, Shantanu leaned across and kissed Shoma, the hot babe he had encountered in London during his conference. He had had a taste of the deceptive pleasures of infidelity and now knew why men and women cheated. Shoma, for one, could do things that he didn't know women were capable of. Using his formidable charm, he had convinced her to accompany him back to India for a brief holiday. She would stay at the Tolly, of course, in Room 502.

■

Blame it on the Generation Gap

'Why have you put ketchup in my sandwich? I specifically told you to use chilli sauce, no ketchup.'

'Sorry, but Mom wanted ketchup and I have only two hands, I can't do everything.'

'Oh, God! Are those olives? You know I hate olives!'

'The kids like olives and I can't make separate sandwiches for everyone. Anyway, now my serial is about to begin.'

'Why can't you make separate sandwiches for everyone? What's the big deal? You put olives in one and you don't put them in the other. It's easy.'

'If you think it is that easy, why don't you make them for everybody the next time? I can't cater to everybody's special requests!'

'See, as it is you haven't cooked a proper dinner. I can't eat this sandwich, I need another one.'

'Then make it yourself. Or wait for an hour. When my serials end, I'll make some for you.'

'Why am I expected to do everything around here? I earn, I take care of the finances. Isn't this your job? Can't you do anything right?'

'I do lots of things right, okay! I take care of the house, and the part-timers who work here. *You* try running the house. Nani yaad aa jayegi!'

'Look, you can't do anything right! Only yesterday you screwed up the club admission forms, today this sandwich. And last month, you forgot to pay the phone bill on time and we were charged late fees.'

'I'd asked you to help me with those forms. And you told me about the phone bill only at the last minute. Don't try to blame me!'

'Excuses, excuses… You're always making excuses!'

'It's very easy for you to lord it over your subordinates. Then you come home and expect everyone to jump to your every command. You never help around the house, you just issue orders. And even in office, I've seen you. You just keep delegating work to others. Try doing something yourself for a change!'

'You're so pathetic! You really think I would be where I am if I did nothing? You're delusional. You should get out and try and actually do a job. You wouldn't last a month. It is very easy to just sit on your ass here all day, have maids do all the work, watch TV all day or be on Facebook and then criticize.'

'Don't you dare start calling me names. I'm not pathetic. You are! I was working when I met you. It was *you* who made me stay home and take care of the kids. Don't think too much of yourself.'

'What is this obsession with your bloody serial? Can't you at least look at me when I'm talking to you?'

'You can't decide when I do what. I'm not your bloody secretary.'

'You wouldn't last one day as my secretary, you stupid cow!'

'Stop calling me names, you bastard!'

'Fuck you, bitch! I've had enough of you. You can't do anything. And there's no sex, too.'

'So, is that what all this is about, this tamasha? Just because we haven't had sex for a few days? You're no better than a horny dog!'

'A few days? It's been three goddamn weeks. Three. Whole. Fucking. Weeks.'

'You asshole!'

'You know, I'm out of here, I've had enough. You're a goddamn cock-teaser, nothing else!'

'Motherfucker! If you want to go, go! I've had enough of you too!'

She glares angrily at him, her stubborn face just a few inches away from his, daring him to touch her. He knows that she is trying to provoke him but is in an incandescent rage. He pushes her away. She falls on to the bed. She gets up quickly, hits him on the arm and lunges for his face, her nails outstretched like talons, but he dodges and pushes her back on to the bed again.

When the argument becomes physical, both become silent, as if by unspoken mutual agreement. They've just moved in to a new house, and his mother-in-law is visiting for the first time. And though she is in the guest bedroom, located immediately below theirs, it would be terrible if she could hear them. Their teenaged kids seemed to have noise-cancelling headphones permanently plugged in to their ears—they probably wouldn't hear even the world end around them.

She lunges at him but he grips both her arms and in a vise-like grip. She struggles to free herself. Her T-shirt has slipped off her shoulder, revealing the strap of her bra. When she catches the hunger in his eyes, she hisses angrily, 'You're sick, just a sick, disgusting prick!' She gets one arm free and strikes him across his chest and his face, wherever she can find an opening.

He pushes her back on to the bed but this time he follows her. He climbs on to her, pinning her down with his weight. 'You're hurting me,' she pants, and tries to reach up to his face and score it with her nails. He catches hold of both hands in one of his and, with the other, rips her T-shirt straight down the middle of her chest. He has managed to get hold of one of the straps of her bra as well and pulls it right off, exposing one of her breasts.

'No, no, stop it!' she gasps, but he is now past listening. He puts one hand on her bared breast and squeezes it hard. 'Ouch! Your nails! You're hurting me. Stop!'

He leans over to bite her on the shoulder, knowing how much she hates his habit of leaving love bites where they are most visible. In leaning forward, he overbalances. She manages to find some wriggle room, quickly inserts her hands under his T-shirt and reaches up to his hairy chest. She hooks her fingers and draws them down sharply over his skin. This time, she has drawn blood for sure.

Muffling a pained grunt, he momentarily shifts his weight to flip her over. Pinning both her arms to the small of her back, he shuffles down to the back of her thighs. He pulls down the loose linen pyjamas she usually wears around the house but she commands him to stop.

'Shut the fuck up!' he hisses. He's reached a checkmate. To get her naked, he must heave himself off of her. But if he moves, there is no telling what she will do. After a momentary hesitation, he finds a solution. He rips her favourite pyjamas and forcibly yanks her panties off. His violence leaves a red welt on her hip.

He eases off a bit, and she turns around. Both of them eye each other warily, taken aback by the violence of the moment they've just shared. With a wicked smile, she slides her hand up the bunched-up muscle of his thigh, through the loose sleeve of the boxers he wears around the house, slips the tips of her fingers under the elastic of his brief and wraps her hand around his cock. His eyes glint in the anticipation of pleasure and she can feel his blood surge. With a sense of delivering just deserts, she squeezes his penis, applying all the force her long fingers and strong wrist can muster.

He winces and almost shouts, but catches himself just in time. 'You fucking bitch!'

She removes her hand, laughing vindictively, which infuriates him even further. He roughly pins her down on her stomach and regains his earlier position of dominance. With one hand he tries to push away the ripped tatters of her clothes and with the fingers of the other—the tips of which he perfunctorily wets with saliva—he probes.

'No, not that. Please, stop, not that…' she howls into the pillow, but he is implacable. He inserts his middle digit deep without any further lubrication. He uses one heavy knee to spread her legs and the further apart they move, the deeper he goes. Her moans are now intertwined notes of pain and pleasure. He pulls his finger out, giving her temporary relief, but sticks it back into her vagina. This time, her almost involuntary gasp is one purely of pleasure. Sensing her relief, he pulls out the middle digit and, combining it with his forefinger, sticks both deep into her. He judges from how easily both his fingers have slid inside, and her heavy breathing, that she is ready. He roughly pulls her up by the hip, so that she is high enough for him to reach her when he is on his knees. Without stopping a moment, he plunges into her. For a moment, she nearly gives in to the force of his penetration but rallies and rocks back on her knees, demanding her pleasure. She reaches her arm around behind her and clenches his hip, pulling him deep.

But when he gets on his feet and the force of his thrust increases, she says between gasps, 'It's hurt...hurting a little...' He immediately stops and withdraws. She turns over on her own, hold her legs aloft and guides him inside.

Holding her ankles for support and to keep her legs apart, he proceeds to pump her hard. She can feel his penis begin to throb within a few minutes. 'Don't come inside me...' He stops and waits for a few seconds, regaining his composure and then starts again. She responds even more keenly when she realizes that he is now on his second wind. By the time he spurts on to her stomach, he has made her a happy woman many times over.

Spent, they both cuddle for a while, nuzzling and kissing each other before drifting off into a comfortable slumber.

■

The next morning, they get up late. Whenever her mom is in

town, it is she who packs the kids off to school so that they can sleep late. As they take a leisurely shower together and change, they discuss the day ahead. She plans to take her mom shopping to the mall where he might join them later. They walk downstairs hand in hand to find breakfast laid out. And her mother is fully dressed to go out and even has her travel bags lined up neatly by the dining table. Her eyes are red from crying.

When she sees them walk down the stairs hand in hand, her face registers shock. Weren't they violently arguing the night before? And using the sort of language she hadn't ever heard anyone use before? How were they together now? And how could they pretend as if nothing had happened? By then, she had taken the precaution of calling up her husband—who had immediately booked her on an earlier flight home—and had prepared him for the possibility that their daughter might be joining them soon, and that too for good.

Her son-in-law is the first one to burst out laughing; her daughter joins in soon after. Over many calming cups of tea, they explain to her that this is but natural for them and for most modern couples. The stresses of life sometimes give rise to outbursts; they are perfectly natural. Of course, they would take care in the future, her daughter said. They had just moved into the new house and had not realized that in the guest bedroom, located directly below theirs, one could hear everything.

Didn't they worry about the kids hearing them fight? They looked sheepishly at each other and confessed that they had checked and knew for sure that no sound was audible in the kids' room, located as it was on the opposite side of the house. And though his mother-in-law could not get how such a vicious fight could be a way for them to release pressure, they prevailed upon her to blame the generation gap for not understanding.

When she finally agrees to stay on, and considers the matter closed, they both heave sighs of relief. For a while they had convinced her about why they fought, how could they have explained to her the way in which they had made up?

The Condom Chronicles

They hadn't yet consummated their relationship. She insisted on condoms and he kept forgetting to carry any. They had had three opportunities to have sex. The first two times, she had begged off, coy about having sex on just their fifth and sixth dates. The third time, when both had mutually decided that they had dated enough, matters halted when she had drawn her Laxman Rekha at the condom. No amount of pleading had been able to persuade her to cross the line. And everyone knows that even the best oral sex can never be a substitute for the real thing.

Over the years, his Misadventures with the Sheath had been the subject of numerous joke sessions with his gang of friends. There was the first time when he had struggled with the rubber, torn it in his haste and had been terrified that his then girlfriend would back out. He still remembers his relief at finding out that she had been as impatient as him to bash on regardless. The next time, again with her, she had turned the light on and his erection had suffered in the process of a long-drawn-out discussion on what the correct method of slipping it on was. There hadn't been a third time. Until today.

■

In the morning, he had received a message from her which told him, in no uncertain terms, to shower and get his clean, Cinthol-scented ass to her place by 8 p.m. He had immediately rushed out to buy a variety of condoms. Abandoning flavour, he had concentrated instead on texture. He also forsook the cheap, unreliable Chinese brands and went, instead, for the steadfast Indian brands and their amazing product range. There were the ribbed, dotted and ultra-thin varieties; something called Long Lasting and something else called Max, which was a combination of all of the above and at a price to match. He had bought a three-pack of all of them. His lack of concern for the expense was a measure of how much he wanted her.

In the bathroom, he had revived his morning wood, stroking it quickly to its engorged glory and had tried each one by one, attempting to get, as it were, a handle on things. He soon began to feel that he would be able to handle any situation quite well. The exercise had been worth the effort and having to endure his parents bang on the door of the bathroom, berating him for holding everyone up. After all, he had the 'Be there at 8' SMS to inspire him.

In the evening, ignoring his mother's heated protests ('Saara paani khatam ho jayega!') he took a leisurely shower, generously applied his father's cologne, and slid out before either of his parents could comment on the perfume cloud which surrounded him. From the reactions of his co-passengers in the lift, he could tell that the cloud was very much on him as he ascended to her flat. He pressed the doorbell and was dragged in before the echo of the bell had subsided.

'Are you hard?' she whispered as he looked around her room in awe. She had lit candles and turned off all the lights. Gauzy curtains billowed in a gentle, warm breeze. She came close, placed one hand on his crotch and paused. She turned up her delicate nose to ask, 'Is that Old Spice you're wearing? It reminds me of my grandfather.' She must have felt him soften because she abruptly abandoned her line of enquiry.

He then whipped out a condom from his back pocket just as she placed an array of gels, her contribution to the night, on the bedside table. She ignored his assurances that he had everything under control—even his brief descriptions of his experiments of the morning. She couldn't bear another failure, she told him. She had checked on the Internet, she said, and these gels, applied to his thing, would help him achieve and maintain an erection. She also reasoned that the extra lubrication would make slipping on the rubber sheath easy. Even as she was explaining all of this to him, she unfastened his trousers, unzipped him, and pulled his pants and briefs to his ankles. By the time she finished, and before he could gather his thoughts to make a coherent response, she had both her hands wrapped around his organ.

The first sign that she might not have conducted as much research as he had was when she struggled to open a sachet containing the gel. She first used her hands, then her nails, and then her teeth before appealing to him. He gave it his all, too, but eventually a trip to the kitchen and the use of a sharp knife was needed. Luckily, he stayed erect throughout. She poured a generous dollop of the gel on to her hands and then on to his flagstaff. She now vigorously rubbed the gel in, taking care not to leave any spot dry. For a few seconds after she had finished, he could feel nothing. Then, an incredibly cold wave started at the tip and travelled down his shaft. By the time she unwrapped the condom he had handed to her, his nether regions felt like they had been exposed to an Arctic blast.

His first choice had been the Ultra-Thins—they had suited him best. He had bought a pack of three, one of which he had already experimented with in the morning. In handling the remaining two, she tore them both within a few seconds of each other. Long, sharpened nails and Ultra-Thins do not go well together. (And since this little fact is not mentioned on the condom packet, a court case is waiting to happen somewhere.) He then took out the Long Lasting variety. This time, he insisted on putting them on himself. If she tore them, he would have none left. (He, obviously, hadn't brought along his entire stock. Even he couldn't go that many times, he knew.) She had by now removed all her clothes in eager anticipation and was lying in bed, clad only panties—black, satin. Just as he began to roll the condom on, he realized that the icy feeling was gradually being replaced by heat. By the time he lay down by her side, the heat had become a raging furnace. Basic science lessons from school told him that the condom was acting as the perfect insulator.

The heat brought to his mind an incident from childhood. Kneed in the groin by a particularly nasty defender, he had gone home and applied Tiger Balm to his peepee. The agony he felt now came very close to what he had felt after the soccer match. He could still see himself sitting inside their tiny bathroom on an upturned bucket, tears rolling down his cheeks, unable to scream or even to sob aloud.

He paused, his dick on fire, while she lay with her legs spread—by now even the black panties had come off. 'What's wrong?' she asked when she saw the first teardrop slide down his cheek. He took a deep breath and then whipped the condom off. His flagstaff didn't take too kindly to it. When his skin came into contact with air, he felt as if a firebomb had gone off in his groin.

'My dick is on fire,' he screamed and began rolling on the bed.

■

They eventually had sex. On that night itself. She first washed him with soap and lots of care, applied ice packs to his beleaguered organ and, when all the ice in the house had melted, used a chilled Pepsi bottle wrapped in cloth. Surprisingly, all her ministrations revived his erection to its full glory. He carefully rolled on his last remaining condom and they began to make love.

They started with the missionary position on her bed and then did it doggy-style on the floor. In the living room she rode him. They ended in the lotus position, back in the bedroom where it had all begun.

He had his eyes closed most of the time, moving with the urgency of a crankshaft working at top speed, and at the same, unvarying pace. She moved around a fair bit, making sure he reached the innermost parts, parts even she wasn't sure existed. She was already sore by the time they reached the living room but he didn't stop. She got back by making sure that every time she used her teeth or nails, they hurt and left a mark. He came in the lotus position in the bedroom, pushed over the edge, finally, when she whispered sweet-nothings urgently into his ear and nibbled his lobes. His pole was feeling quite hot—though for an entirely different reason this time—when he pulled out of her and peeled off the exhausted condom.

■

None of their subsequent sessions matched up to their first. She even let herself be persuaded to be fucked bareback but though that worked for him, it didn't for her. They broke up a couple of months later after their relationship fell victim to the once-in-a-lifetime-experience which could never be matched.

He still swears by that particular Indian brand of condoms. And on some dates he carries a sachet of the gel with him, just to keep the memory alive. But he has never managed to work up enough courage to actually try it once again.

■

The Mice Shall Play

They were both in their bedrooms, talking to each other on the phone. The air conditioners were blasting at full power, the doors were shut, and both the television sets were set to the same channel. Even though it was only just after noon, Manoj was delicately sipping on a large McClelland, and trying to get Malti to correctly pronounce the name.

He gave up after the fourth attempt. 'Arre Malti ji, rehne di jiye. Yeh jaam aapke naam hi to hai, kya farak padta hai? Iss serial ke baare mein bataiye. Humein to kuch samajh hi nahin aa raha hai, kaun ab kiske saath hai.' He put an eye-mask on and lay back on the pillows as he listened to her long, involved explanation. He knew that as she brought him up to speed on the serial, she would be sipping on her vodka and orange juice, which she would have made with lots of ice, just the way she liked it.

After a few minutes of small talk, Manoj asked the question Malti had been waiting for, and which brought a bright smile to her face. 'Toh aaj aapne kya pehna hua hai, Madam Malti? Thoda vistaar mein bataiye.'

She decided to be coy and asked him to go first. 'Oho,' he said, 'iss naacheez ke vastra jaan ke kya karengi aap? Khair batate hain. Par pehle zara whisky ka refill kar aayein.' He cradled the cordless phone with his shoulder and walked leisurely to the bar, took the key out from its hiding place and examined the impressive array of bottles. 'Oho, sirf ek aur single malt rahti hai. Glenmorangie. Dekhiye, aap rehne dein, aapse naam nahin bola jayega.' He poured himself a peg. 'Arre nahin, McClelland to kaafi bachi hai, Malti ji, par aapko hamara usool pata hi hai: Ek time pe, ek peg se zyaada, ek bottle se nahin. Khair, aap ne screwdriver Absolut se banayi hai ya Belvedere se?' he asked as he walked back to the room. 'Kya? Grey Goose se? Kya baat hai, Malti ji, aapka status to bas aur ooncha hota hi chala ja raha hai.'

He shut the bedroom door behind him and sprawled out on the bed. 'Kuch der ab hamara programme dekh lein? VH1 lagaiye toh. Channel 703 hai, Tata Sky pe. Arre, aap se kitni baar kaha hai, Airtel chhod dijiye, Tata Sky lagwa lijiye. Khair, music channels mein dhoondhiye. Rihanna ka aaj kal mein naya gaana release hone wala hai. Bhagwan ne unhe bhi badi fursat mein banaya hai.' Realizing his misstep, he quickly back-tracked, 'Mujhe toh lagta hai ki aap ko bhi aise video banana shuru kar dena chahiye. Phir Rihanna rahengi bahar walon ke liye, Bharat mein to sirf aap ki chalegi!'

On hearing her giggle, he switched topics again. 'Toh hum ne pehna hai purple dressing gown, wahi wala jo aapko pasand hai. Uske neeche, Abercombie and Fitch ki T-shirt. Aur neeche… Aur neeche, aapka manpasand, lal wala Calvin Klein ka underwear. Ab aapki baari.' He lay back on the pillow again, put his feet up and closed his eyes meditatively. She was wearing that yellow towel robe, she said, and a matching yellow lace bra beneath that. Of course, the robe was open at the top to showcase the bra and what it held. He sighed slowly, imagining her dusky skin set off by the yellow bra. His hand snaked towards his crotch, under the robe.

But when she described her panties, he sat up and pulled off the eye mask. 'Malti ji, yeh to hamare agreement ke khilaaf hai. Yeh to saaf baat hui thi ki aap woh pink wali patli panty, sirf jab hum honge tab pehnengi. Yeh to gair kanooni hai, aur iski saza hum aapko zaroor denge!' Just as he was about to spell out to Malti the terms of her punishment, he heard a commotion at the main gate of the house. He looked out from the window and said urgently to Malti, 'Arre, memsahib wapas aa gayi hain. Bye, baad mein baat karte hain.'

Manoj was a very busy man for the next five minutes. He quickly switched the air conditioner off, stripped off the gown, T-shirt and underwear, neatly folded all of them and placed each in its appointed place. He then put his simple white uniform on, downed the rest of the Glenmorangie, rinsed his mouth, popped an elaichi to mask the smell, and ran to the door to open it before Madam had to ring the doorbell a second time.

'Namaste Madam ji, aaj aap jaldi aa gaye, achcha hai,' he said, moving quickly to stop the driver outside the door. 'Tum yeh hamein de do,' he said, taking all the bags from the man's hand and then summarily shut the door in his face. He then turned around and hurried off, reaching the bedroom before Madam could. By the time Madam had sat on the bed, he had stowed the bags away and had switched on the AC. 'Paani lengi, Madam?' he asked, and rushed off to the kitchen without waiting for a reply, returning with a glass of half-chilled, half-room temperature water, just the way Madam liked it. 'Aapke liye chai bhi chadha di hai, Madam. Kya aap lunch lengi?' On seeing her shake her head, he returned to the kitchen, where he first rinsed the glass he had been drinking from and placed it back in the bar, using the hidden key to first unlock and then lock it.

When he heard the door to Madam's bathroom shut, he risked a quick phone call to Malti to let her know that everything was under control. Else he knew that she would worry unnecessarily and possibly do something stupid. 'Manoj!' Madam called out. As he walked to the bedroom, he thought how difficult it was to live with women or live without them.

'Manoj. Chai rehne do, make me a Cosmopolitan. Tumhein pata hai na kaise banate hain?'

'Madam, ek baar aur bata dijiye, humein yaad nahin rahta,' he said, flinching at her exasperated cry.

Then, as he walked out, he said, 'Madam, zara bar bhi khol dijiye.'

'Khud hi khol lo. Tumhein pata hi hai chabi kahan rakhhi hai.'

He shook his head regretfully, keeping his eyes lowered. 'Nahin, madam, humein nahin pata bar ki chabi kahan hai. Aap to jaanti hain, humein ismein dilchaspi nahin hai.' He preferred to keep things this way, to let them think that he was slightly dim.

He looked away appropriately while she hunted for the hidden key. A few minutes later, she was smacking her lips appreciatively as she sipped the expertly prepared Cosmopolitan. 'Manoj, tum drinks to bahut mast banate ho. Tumhein barman hona chahhiye.'

He handed her a plate of seekh kebabs. 'Nahin, nahin,' she shrieked. 'Main lunch kar ke aayi hoon.'

'Bas ek try kijiye, naye tareeke se banaya hai,' he said, leaving the plate by her bedside. As he left the room, Madam gave him her ATM debit card and asked him to withdraw ten thousand rupees. She then lay down on the same side of the bed he had been sprawling on a short while ago. When he returned a half hour later, he came prepared with the cocktail shaker in his hand. Sure enough, she wanted a refill and smiled at him as he poured her a second drink. The plate of kebabs, as expected, was empty too. She then briefly told him about the guests they were expecting for dinner and they discussed the menu, agreeing on a set of dishes based on what was available and what was possible. As he was leaving, she asked him to switch the light off before shutting the bedroom door behind him.

He waited for fifteen minutes and then tiptoed to the bedroom door. When he put his ear to the door, he could hear her snoring loudly. He picked up the cordless phone and dialled Malti. She had it easier because the couple she worked for both had day jobs and she was pretty much the queen of the house till her employers returned, which was usually late. Malti picked up the phone just as visions of her dusky, pert ass in the flimsy pink panties were flooding his mind. He retired to his quarters. As she giggled and picked up the thread of conversation which had been interrupted by Madam's arrival, his hand started working furiously inside his trousers. He ejaculated within a few minutes and then they started talking of other, more important matters.

■

The next morning, it was 9 a.m. by the time he finished clearing up the previous night's dinner mess. As always, he marvelled at the amount of food and drink these people could put away. That Mrs Khanna, for instance, could probably eat more than even Bhola who, everyone knew, was the undisputed glutton of their village.

Sir left for office by 10:30 a.m., his usual time, just as Madam called for her bed tea. She had to attend a meeting of the Rotary Club and his plans had been laid out accordingly. She came to the table for breakfast at around 11:00 a.m., running late as usual for her meeting, which began at 11:30. She asked Manoj to rush out and withdraw another ten thousand rupees while she ate. She'd forgotten she had to pay her friend for their last kitty. Near the door, Manoj turned around and said casually, 'Madam, peeche se humein thodi der ke liye bahar jaana hoga. Hamare rishtedar aaye hain gaon se, unhein milne jayenge.'

Madam's eyes narrowed. 'Kitni der ke liye? Kahan jaoge?'

He said patiently, 'Bas ek ghante ke liye, takreeban do-teen baje. Yahin paas mein, ek bhai ke yahan thahre huay hain.' He could never understand this. If she wasn't home, surely he had the freedom to go wherever he wanted to if work wasn't affected?

Madam grudgingly grunted her approval.

He had another request. 'Madam, zara security guard ko bhi bol dijiyega. Nahin toh woh Gurkha bahut tang karta hai.' He had never got along with the new security guard, the tiny man from Nepal, who eyed everyone with suspicion and preferred to keep to himself.

As Madam's car pulled out of the driveway, he watched from the window as she paused at the gate to instruct the security guard, who kept turning to look up at him.

■

At around 1 p.m., the doorbell rang. It was the security guard. There was a salesgirl, he said, carrying two big boxes, who insisted that she had an appointment with Madam. She demanded that she be let in even after being told that Madam wasn't home. Could Manoj deal with her?

Manoj patiently heard the girl out and then called Madam from his mobile. He spoke in a low voice, but did not move out of the guard's hearing. 'Madam, sorry to disturb, ek vacuum cleaner company se Miss Mayawati aayi hain, keh rahin hain ke appointment hai. Keh rahin hain hamein vacuum cleaner ka demo dekar ek hafte ke trial ke liye chhod jayengi. Hamara toh cleaner do mahine se kharab pada hai, hum soch rahe the yeh try kar lete hain.'

He then hung up, smiling at the security guard and the salesgirl. 'Madam ne kaha theek hai. Woh meeting mein hain, zyada baat nahin kar sakti.'

When the guard stiffly said that he should also have been allowed to speak with her, Manoj was curt. 'Toh apne phone se kar lo. Hamara talktime kyun use karoge?'

Manoj knew that the guard didn't have Madam's mobile number and had no option but to go along with what he said.

'Please, aaiye,' he said to the salesgirl, picking up one box and motioning to the guard to pick up the other. 'Demo mein kitna time lagega?' he asked. Her reply, that it would take one to two hours, was loud enough for the guard to hear. He placed the box in the foyer, took the other one from the guard and, after ushering the salesgirl in, shut the door firmly in the guard's face. (He was

Eighteen Plus

the only one allowed inside the house and missed no opportunity to remind the driver and the guard about his elevated status.) He then turned around and embraced the salesgirl warmly. 'Oh, Malti ji! Kitne din ho gaye!'

She giggled as he led her towards the bedroom—where he had had the AC running for the last hour so that the room was suitably cool for her. He also had her favourite drink and snacks laid out. He complimented her on looking stunning in a tight white shirt and jacket, with a matching skirt. It was a typical professional's outfit from her madam's wardrobe. When she told him how much it cost—her madam had bragged to her, she said—he could only stare unbelievingly.

After she had quickly downed her drink, she lay down on the bed and began unbuttoning her dress very, very slowly, one teasing button at a time. As she removed the jacket, she made sure he caught a glimpse of the pink bra.

The sex, as always, was hurried, frantic and passionate. When she took off her shirt, the sight of her breasts drove him mad. Somehow, he found Malti's breasts jiggling in her madam's bra, which was a couple of sizes too large for her, very sexy. As he pulled the skirt down, he could see the miniscule pink panties she wore; the thin strip at the back which passed through the crack of her ass drove him wild with lust.

He roughly shoved his hand down the slim front of the panty and, on feeling her wetness, lost no time in taking her hand and placing it inside his trousers. After she had played with him for a while and used her mouth to fully erect him, she neatly folded her clothes by the side of the bed and lay back naked on it. Manoj immediately took her. Manoj had a small penis but knew how to use it, unlike the driver from the house next to her madam's who was a brute with a huge cock but didn't have Manoj's stamina. Manoj didn't know about the man and she intended to keep it that way.

Having starved for about ten days, Manoj came early but, true to form, he was ready to go within fifteen minutes, timing it perfectly so that she had just finished her second drink when he became hard. They switched positions to her favourite this time, doggy-style—Manoj liked missionary more so that he could see her face and breasts as he fucked her. But doggy-style was good, too. He pulled her by her hair and spread her legs with his to penetrate as deep as he could, withdrawing almost completely each time and then going in fully.

In their last encounter, he had found to his surprise that she had a taste for slightly rough sex. As he kept up his steady strokes, he reached around to handle her breasts harshly and tweak her nipples between his fingers. She groaned in satisfaction first and reached her customary shuddering orgasm. A couple of minutes after that, he came again with a few groans of his own, spraying all over her pert ass, something that he liked doing but she didn't enjoy much. She didn't complain today, though. They both had a quick shower, liberally using the shower gels kept in the bathroom, and got busy with their work. She left at around 2 p.m. with her boxes. Half an hour later, he left as well, carrying a satchel. The guard, out of spite, went through it with a fine-toothed comb and found only dirty clothes.

■

When Madam came home from her meeting, she first screamed,

and then called her husband. Her jewellery was missing and so was all the cash at home. All the valuables which had been kept safely locked away was gone, she blubbered to her husband. Manoj must have found out where the key was hidden and planned it all out. A quick call to the bank confirmed that money was missing from the bank account. When Sir rushed home, and they questioned the security guard, they learnt about the vacuum-cleaner lady. The guard swore Manoj had called Madam to check before he let her in. But Madam vigorously denied it, and her call records didn't show anything as well.

When the police were finally called, the first thing they did was arrest the guard, suspecting collusion. The total amount robbed was disclosed to be one lakh twenty thousand rupees, though, Madam confided to Mrs Khanna later, the real amount was closer to fifteen lakh rupees, which her husband had always kept as an 'emergency cash reserve' at home. The police couldn't be told that, obviously.

Manoj's cruellest cut was revealed in the evening. When Madam and Sir opened the bar late that night to have a consolatory drink, they found that their entire collection of vodkas and single malts had disappeared. There was a 'thank you' note in its place, along with a detailed recipe for the perfect Cosmopolitan.

■

Two Days in a Nerd's Life

He was in heaven. The ceaseless toil of the last few years was finally paying off. He had been chosen from among the thirty-six thousand employees of the company—well, nineteen thousand if one considered only the Bangalore-based ones—to demonstrate, and then hand over, the programme to the clients in Goa. He was under no illusions as to how it had come about. He knew he had to thank the virus which had afflicted his boss, as well as his super boss' love for pani puri which had rendered him immobile with stomach cramps.

But then, he reasoned, they could have chosen anyone else from the project team. Why him? It was obvious! He had slogged his ass off the last few years developing the programme, and he was the most discreet, safest member of the team. Who better than him to deliver the programme to the US-based group—currently in a conference in Goa—to whom they had sold it for a million dollars? The good times were about to begin. He could feel it in his bones. The astrologer had told his mom so. His mother had told him. And she was never wrong. It was his time now!

■

On the flight to Goa, the feeling in his bones became stronger. The one thing all men fantasize about happened to him. The sexiest woman he had ever seen in real life—not counting the brief glimpse of Sunny Leone when she had visited their building to attend a promotional event at the radio station upstairs—had entered the plane and made her way to the seat next to him. She was wearing a really short, tight skirt, with a slit down the side which revealed her milky-white inner thigh as she crossed her legs. The top two buttons of her form-fitting white shirt were open. Her breasts strained to escape the confines of her bra, the red, lacy edge of which was visible under the open collar of her white shirt. He could feel the lust and envy which came off every man on the plane in waves. She turned to him, delicately held out a hand, and introduced herself.

Naturally, they began talking. But this weird song, in which Katrina Kaif kept begging a man to 'zara zara touch me, touch me, touch me; zara zara hold me, hold me, hold me' kept interrupting his conversation with the angel next to him. He really wished people would switch their mobiles off, especially on a plane. And what a horrible song for a ringtone! Such a tasteless, vulgar item number! It took three missed calls for him to figure out, more from her expression than from anything else, that it was his phone which was playing this abomination. His office, due to the nature of secretive work they did, was a strict, no-mobile-allowed zone. And not many people called him anyway. Silently cursing his neighbour's son for changing his ringtone, he connected with the caller. His boss, he informed her and the air hostess who came to request him to switch the phone off. Yes, he had boarded. Yes, everything was okay. Yes, the memory stick was in his possession. Yes, he knew how much it was worth. Yes, it was definitely in his possession right now. No, he was certain, he didn't have to check in his baggage. Yes, he would call as soon as he landed. Switching the phone off, he turned once more to his co-passenger.

■

He waited by the conveyor belt to assist her with her bag. Even she was here just for a day, she had confided to him on the plane, leaning forward so that the top of her creamy white breasts, attractively set off by the red of her bra, were visible. He called up his boss to inform him that he had landed. The super boss was on the call as well. 'Do not fuck this up' was the loud and clear message that was conveyed to him. After assuring them both that all was under control, he switched the phone off.

By some heavenly coincidence, they were staying at the same hotel. They agreed to meet for coffee at 6:00 in the lobby, giving her a chance to freshen up and for him to run the programme once to make sure that it was in perfect order. When they met, she suggested some wine. He—despite much persuasion and several glimpses of her perfectly flat stomach, which was revealed every time she reached up to adjust her hair, and her too-short T-shirt rode up her midriff—stuck to water. He didn't drink juice, tea, coffee. He definitely didn't indulge in hard drink and positively ate no non-vegetarian food. This was a promise that he had made to his mother when he left home in their small village to come to Bangalore. Nothing was going to sway him. He told her all this with a smile, hoping that she would understand, and cringed inwardly when he saw her face fall. He hoped his restrictions wouldn't come in the way of a pleasant evening. For he loved the attention that their table was getting. This veritable goddess was inexplicably paying him, a garden-variety nerd, complete attention and he just could not believe it. For one precarious second, he even thought of breaking his vow but then he dismissed the thought immediately; he couldn't ever disobey his mother.

After that momentary disappointment, his dinner date became cheerful again. She flashed a smile at him and uncrossed and re-crossed her legs. Somehow, the skinny jeans which lovingly hugged her shapely legs gave them so much more allure. She went ahead, though, and drank two glasses of white wine. Just as he was thinking of what they should do for dinner, she suggested that they go to his room and order from room service.

The astrologer's prediction, which once seemed near-unlikely, had just become a certainty.

■

She pounced on him as soon as they entered the room, and pressing him against the wall, kissed him with aggression, thrusting her tongue deep into his mouth. He was taken aback by the ferocity of her attack. She then took a step a back and in two swift, practised movements slipped the T-shirt over her head and peeled off the skinny jeans. She then kissed him again, crushing her breasts against his chest. She took his hands and guided them back, over her buttocks, urging him to press her against him.

He stood there, unmoving, unbelieving, as she let go of his

hands and expertly undid his belt, the clasps of his trousers and unzipped him. The garment fell in a heap around his ankles. She then reached inside his briefs. He could see her eyes widen in amazement as her fingers wrapped around his girth and, when she pulled him out, an involuntary exclamation escaped her when she saw the actual size of his massive penis. It was almost as if she had expected something modest, given his personality. She then dropped down to her knees in front of him with the air of a devout. For a moment, he thought she couldn't manage it, but she wrapped both her hands around the base of his shaft, opened wide, and took him all in. He could feel his eyes roll up into the back of his skull. He had never imagined that this could be so pleasurable. In a while, she stopped, stood up and pressed down on his shoulders until he lay down on the carpet. She took her panties off and threw them to the side. She unclasped her bra, took it off, and tied his hands over his head with it. Stopping briefly to carefully ease him into her, she began to ride him. She rocked slowly at first, but soon gathered speed. He simply lay still, gazing up at her wonderful breasts as they bounced about in rhythm. As she rocked back on his cock, her nipples jumped, reached the apex of their trajectory, and plunged down when she rocked forward. The back and forth gained in intensity until, finally, she reached back, gripped his thighs, arched her back, and came. He simply stared in wonder as she moaned and grunted in endless, shuddering ecstasy.

After her monster orgasm, she climbed off him and he got up. She then kneeled before him, alternately wrapping her lips and her hands around his cock until he, within minutes, spurted cum all over the carpet. What a fantastic first time he'd just had!

The very stuff of fantasies. Enjoying the afterglow in each other's arms, she tried once more to convince him to order some wine. And although he was besotted with her by now, he politely declined.

She then got into bed, yawning widely, and invited him to spoon with her, naked. He jumped at the opportunity. She fell asleep promptly, but he remained wide awake, a beatific smile plastered on his face.

When her sleep broke at around midnight, she found that she had been woken by his erection knocking persistently on her backdoor. They started just the way they were, in the spoon position, before she got to her knees. Even though he was behind her, she controlled the pace of their lovemaking; he was too engrossed in his pleasure to take charge. He lasted a very long while, and she had many multiple orgasms before he squirted all over her back. She fell promptly asleep again; he was too dazed by what was happening to him to even contemplate slumber.

Around 5 a.m., despite her best efforts to feign sleep, he put her in a state of boil by finding her clitoris. He then found her breasts and she taught him to apply his tongue everywhere. Then they showered together, and made love standing. Dawn found them in bed, lying side by side.

■

At breakfast, he wanted to propose marriage to her. That was how happy he was. He, quite extravagantly, ordered from room service all the sweet items on the menu: pancakes, waffles, French toast. At one point she had professed a sweet tooth. He was single, she was single. They were perfect together. Hadn't she praised him for his solid nature, his calmness, for his feet which were planted firmly on the ground? Hadn't she confessed to her own impulsiveness, recklessness and dreaminess? Without saying the actual words, she had implied that she needed someone like him in her life. She even had long hair, he noted, the kind his mom wanted her daughter-in-law to keep. He was sure she would approve.

Oh, God! Someone in the hotel was playing that item number from the plane. Was there no escape? Was tastelessness truly the norm now? And why did it have to interrupt their breakfast? Again, it took him a couple of minutes to figure out that the abominable ringtone came from his phone. His super boss was on the line. Yes, he was fine. Yes, the programme was in his possession. Yes, he knew how much it was worth. Yes, he knew where he had to go to give the demo. Yes, he knew what time, he was in touch with the buyers. Before hanging up, he thanked his super boss for showing faith in him, promised him that he wouldn't let him down and then hung up. He had always thought the super boss had a very low opinion of him, he had always thought him to be an idiot, he said to her. Obviously, he was wrong.

■

After breakfast, they went back to his room. She astounded him by wriggling her bra out through her shirt sleeve. He had never seen it done before and it turned him on immensely. She suggested that they do it one more time before his meeting. He looked at her, then at his watch, and decided that they could, indeed, and he'd have enough time later for a shower. The early morning shower, after all, had been severely compromised. Much surer of himself now, he pulled her shirt over her head and admired her breasts as they jiggled freely. He nibbled at her nipples and then slid down the front of her trousers, under the elastic band of her panties and placing his hand over her pussy, basked in the heat that it gave off.

She then sat on a low stool. He kneeled before her and unfastened her trousers blindly, for his face was buried in her breasts. Since last night, he must have kissed, licked, sucked, teased, nibbled, bitten them a hundred times but he couldn't get enough. He was convinced that he never would. Never taking his attention off her magnificent melons for even a second, he boosted her off the chair for a few seconds and slid her trousers—and the panties along with it—off. As he stood in front of her, he expected her to rip his trousers off, to take him in her mouth, but strangely, the fervour of the previous night was missing. She, who had taken charge so eagerly, seemed content to be led. Oh well, he thought as he peeled off his trousers and entered her, still on his knees.

After she had come twice, he slid her off the stool, on to the carpet, and penetrated her sideways. He couldn't see it, but her eyes were closed and she seemed to be willing herself to go on. Mercifully, he came soon, this time inside her. She turned around to face him and sincerely complimented his stamina and staying power. He was inordinately pleased. Then, realizing the time, he rushed off to the bathroom.

■

He looked at himself in the mirror. He was meeting the buyers in the hotel lobby and he would be there comfortably on time. The demo wouldn't take more than a couple of hours, including questions. So he could be back by four, time enough for one more session before she left for her evening flight. He was booked to travel the next morning. The quicker the meeting ended, the more time they had for one more quickie, was his last thought as he straightened his tie and stepped out into the room.

■

She had left. And had taken every trace of herself along. He quickly rummaged through his bag. The memory stick, which was labelled PROGRAMME, too, was missing. So this was what all of this had been about: industrial sabotage. He sat on the bed, his head spinning. He was disappointed, distraught. The atrocious ringtone sounded again; it was his boss. He ignored it.

■

After she had walked out of the hotel and boarded a cab to the airport, she placed a call to his super boss. She confirmed that she had the memory stick in her possession, but her price would be triple the agreed amount. Once the apoplectic reaction at the opposite end had subsided, she calmly explained. First, he hadn't told her that the man was a teetotaler. How could she spike his drink, then? And the agreement had been for one fuck, tops. He'd gone all night, she hadn't slept a wink and he had left her exhausted. Yes, of course she had enjoyed it, but that wasn't the point. She reminded him of all the money he was going to make selling the programme on the open market and advised him to be generous. He reluctantly agreed to her terms.

He curtly told her to hurry up and catch her flight but was smiling as he put down the phone. He had done it. He had dodged all the internal security and secured a copy of the entire programme for himself, which was worth a fortune on the open market. And he had a scapegoat, too.

■

After the scapegoat got over his initial disappointment, he looked around the room more carefully. Near the door, beside a cupboard, he found one of her panties. She must have forgotten it in her rush to leave. He smiled as he remembered the pleasant shock of the night before, when she had first jumped him. He picked up the panty; it would make a nice keepsake.

His mother had a saying: If something is too good to be true, it usually is. He mentally thanked his mother and her canny wisdom. In the aeroplane, as well as in the hotel, despite the amazing things that were happening to him, he had never fully understood why such a smoking-hot babe should throw herself at him. And that had bothered him. He was under no illusions about his nerd-hood.

His phone rang again but he ignored it. (He made a mental note to change the ringtone soon after the meeting ended.) It was his boss, yet again. He suspected that either of the two, or both, must surely be involved in this deception, since only they were in the loop about his travel plans. But there would be time enough to investigate that later. Now, he had to proceed to the meeting.

After dressing up for the meeting, he carefully inserted two fingers into the secret pocket which was sewn into his trouser waistband and fished out a plain, unlabelled memory stick. This was another habit which had been inculcated by his mother. Ever since he had been a school-going child, his mother had taught him to keep his valuables, lunch money and suchlike, in his secret pocket. And she had sewn those pockets into all of his trousers.

As he reached across the table to shake the buyers' hands and seal the deal, he grinned. Who could have thought that industrial sabotage could be so fun and satisfying. And what fantastic sex he'd had in the last two days!

■

The Memoir of a Sexologist

It is not easy to be a sexologist in India. Most men have such giant egos that they refuse to even consider the possibility that there could be something wrong with their manhood. Or that they could need help with something related to sex. These are the same men, mind you, who have no problem eating bulls' testicles cooked in the blood of a rooster or something equally vile if a friend tells them that it will increase their virility. Though they will happily send their womenfolk for multiple check-ups. Again and again. And to several doctors. Only female doctors, though. Which is why I made my wife, who is also a qualified sexologist, practise with me in our clinic after our two kids had grown up. But I'm telling this story very badly. All this has nothing to do with what happened. Well, almost nothing.

■

It was a dark and stormy night. I have always wanted to start a story with these words. But I digress.

Actually, it was actually dark and stormy. We had begun shutting our clinic down when, at 8 p.m., the phone rang. A gruff voice asked for me in the harsh Haryanvi accent which is commonly used by the people who live in our area. When I said it was me on the line, he asked for my wife, completely mangling her name I confirmed her presence and asked him for his name, but the man disconnected. When we stepped out of our clinic after shutting it down, we saw six men waiting by the doorway, all draped in black shawls. Two of them were carrying guns and another two were carrying scotch tape. In minutes they put the tape on our mouths, trussed up our hands and feet and bundled us into the back seat of a SUV. There they placed a black hood over our heads.

My first thought was that we were being kidnapped. It is quite common in our area, Bahadurgarh, which falls on the border between Delhi and Haryana. The modus operandi of the kidnappers is simple: ask for a very high ransom, settle for about twenty per cent of the original demand, and then release the captors. (Yes, Indians negotiate everything, including ransom. I've had patients negotiate the fees for surgical operations, at times after they've been performed.) Usually, no one goes to the police who are after their own cut. So far, all the kidnapees from our area have been released and there have been no murders, so there was nothing really to worry about. But I could still feel my heart rate pushing 160 bpm.

We arrived at our destination in just over fifteen minutes. Our hoods were removed and we stepped out of the car into a courtyard-cum-driveway. The courtyard had a massive lawn and half a dozen cars were parked on the driveway. A wall, ten or fifteen feet high, surrounded the entire property, and the barbed wire on top of the fence seemed electrified. My heart sank. Seeing the swankiness of the place, I mentally doubled the amount I had estimated we would end up paying. That was when I spotted the two guards at the entrance of the house, both carrying machine guns. This was turning out to be a really slick kidnapping operation. I glumly shook my head; to make the ransom, we would probably have to sell the land that we bought in nearby Sampla a few years ago.

Once inside, they loosened our bonds and sat us down on sofas in a gigantic living room which looked like it could easily double up as a set for any one of the Hindi serials which are broadcast at primetime. The marble used in the room alone would have emptied out at least a few quarries. They all obviously treated their victims well since tea arrived a few minutes after we were ushered in. But the six goons who had picked us up all stood around us, watching grimly. Then my wife shocked me by asking for biscuits. Which, even more shockingly, arrived promptly. Here I was, shitting bricks, and there she was, peacefully dunking her biscuits in her tea. But then she is a Bengali in the Ma Durga mould. There is very little in this world which can faze her.

Just as I was beginning to wonder what all this was about, Tauji arrived. Tauji is one of the more popular, more rustic, politicians of Haryana. He once came close to being the Chief Minister of the state, but he is best known as the longtime kingmaker of Haryana. His image is that of a benevolent yet feared strongman. When I saw him, I multiplied the ransom amount—which I had earlier doubled—by ten.

Tauji settled in, made himself comfortable and bellowed,

'Oye, Chotu kahan mar gaya? Saare Haryana ke choot choos raha hai, bhosadi ke?' Chotu arrived within two seconds.

Tauji now turned to the six goons. 'Tum kyun abhi bhi lund haath mein liye khade ho yahan pe? Bhago, haraamzadon!' Shortly after they'd left, he turned and faced us. Such was his presence that we both shrank back a little.

He then asked us in perfect English, 'Are you comfortable?' The American twang he spoke shocked us so much that I dropped my teacup and even my wife who, as I mentioned, is rarely fazed, looked at him, her mouth agape. His eyes twinkled at our reaction.

'I need your help with a delicate matter,' he continued. 'My younger son has been married now for four months but still can't get his wife pregnant. Useless, both of them!'

'But four months is not long, give them some time,' said my wife. She doesn't know when to keep quiet.

Tauji looked at her with scorn. 'In our family, four months is a very long time! My elder son's wife took two months. I was conceived a month into my father's marriage. And I,' he said with pride, 'got my wife pregnant just fifteen days into our marriage.'

It was clear that early pregnancy was some kind of badge of honour within the clan.

He continued, 'I want you to conduct a full medical check-up on both of them. Most medical reports are already available but if you need anything else, the hospital next door belongs to me. Anything, any time; you just have to ask. Chotu,' he gestured to his elder son, 'will organize everything. I am leaving for my hometown and will come back tomorrow. I expect you to have sorted everything out by then.'

'Twenty-four hours! That's just not possible!' exclaimed my wife.

This time Tauji stood up to his full height, a good six feet and a half, tapped his cane on the floor, and said, 'Then make it possible!'

I spoke for the first time. 'Tauji,' I said, 'we don't have our bags, our medical instruments. How can we work?'

'Just write a note to your compounder, make a list, Chotu will go get it.'

It was then that I asked what had been on my mind since he had arrived. 'But why did you bring us here this way? And why us?'

'Do you have any idea what would happen if word leaked that one of Tau's children has a problem? Have you thought what that would do my reputation?' he thundered. 'And what about the upcoming elections? I chose you because you're the only doctor couple in this field within a radius of a hundred kilometres. Chotu checked on Google.' He paused, gazed levelly at us, and said, 'Now, is there anything else?'

'Yes.' My wife was determined to have the last word. 'Can we have Good Day biscuits with our tea instead of the cheap ones we got?'

Tauji turned and left, but not without giving me a withering glance to express his displeasure at my inability to keep my wife under control.

An hour later, our instruments were with us, we'd had another round of tea (this time with Good Day biscuits), and had discussed our approach with Chotu. The plan was to meet the couple, Lambu and Bebe together, then conduct an individual check before reconvening. Some recent blood-test reports were available and they seemed fine.

∎

Lambu, all of five feet four inches, thin and scrawny, sat uncomfortably in front of us. His wife, draped in a long ghoonghat, sat next to him, while we sat in chairs facing them. After fifteen minutes of questioning, we realized that we weren't getting anywhere.

'Have you had sex with each other?' I asked

Lambu answered with a soft, embarrassed, 'Yes,' while Bebe nodded reluctantly.

'Do you enjoy it?' my wife enquired.

There was an even softer 'yes' from Lambu and, after what seemed like a couple of minutes, Bebe also said 'yes.'

'How often do you have sex?'

Lambu almost whispered, 'Three…four,' while Bebe held up three fingers. With great misgiving I asked if they had sex thrice weekly, monthly or in three times in all, but Lambu, with a shy smile, confirmed that it was weekly.

After asking a few more questions and receiving monosyllabic replies and confusing nods of the head, we decided to move to the individual sessions. The memory of Tauji's tapping cane provided us a powerful incentive.

My routine one-on-ones, in which I try to get a sense of the patient's life history, mental make-up and sexual past, wasn't straightforward in Lambu's case. Being the younger one, and the runt of the litter, he had been the over-protected baby of the family and the butt of constant jokes among his cousins. He was shy and had a sensitive personality. He had never watched pornography or visited a prostitute in his life. (This made him the subject of constant ridicule among the men of his clan.) He had been a virgin before his arranged marriage. He liked Bebe, he said. She was even quieter than him, showed the elders of the family proper respect, and did her share of chores without fuss. And as for the sex? Well, umm, it was fine, he said.

It took me an hour of sustained questioning to extract the above information. Not a man of many words, our Lambu.

He said that he had observed bulls, dogs and cats do it. Before marriage, he had been ready and eager, and had even climaxed several times. He had no idea that Bebe could have an orgasm, too. He wasn't aware that women orgasmed, too, and now that he had been told, he was curious how they did. Did she ejaculate like he did? He had no problems with erections and physical examination confirmed the fact quite easily. Our conversation had apparently aroused him.

My wife assured me that my experience had been a cakewalk compared to hers. Bebe was also the youngest child, the only daughter, and had been fiercely guarded by her five brothers. She hadn't been allowed to go to school; certain female teachers had been invited home to teach her some basics for a few years. She wasn't used to speaking and chose to answer most questions with nods. Her mother had warned her that sex hurt and it was true. It still hurt her a bit, but not as much as the first few times, when she had almost passed out from pain. Her physical examination had been cursory since she hadn't cleaned up for ages. My wife is a bit of a stickler on that point. She had handed Bebe a vaginal wash and had told her to scrub herself well before the next session.

Both Bebe and Lambu were given identical instructions: they were to have sex tonight.

■

We had had an eventful day, to say the least, and my wife and I crashed without much trouble. The room we'd been given was nice and comfortable. A tea pot, some Good Day biscuits and several bottles of mineral water had been placed beside the bed. We were woken up at about 3 a.m. by Bebe's screams—partly of pain and partly of pleasure—and Lambu's grunts—louder than many a player on the ATP tour. Steady, rhythmic thudding resounded off one of the walls of the room—their bed was probably hitting against our common wall. It seemed as if Tauji had planned our quarters for the night so that we could monitor our patients' progress. Lambu and Bebe went at it for about half an hour and we stayed awake the entire time. No, we didn't do it during that time. And yes, our sex life is pretty good, compared to most of the couples we speak to, thanks for asking!

■

For breakfast there was some delicious poha which we ate at a huge dining table sitting with Chotu, his wife Badi, Lambu and Bebe.

And shortly after that, we met our two patients individually again.

The sex had been good, Lambu assured me. She had smelt nice. He praised the soap Doctor Memsaab had given Bebe. And everything had happened as normal.

The sex had lasted about ten-fifteen-twenty-twenty-five

minutes. He wasn't really sure. When I told him that we'd heard the entire performance and had timed it at twenty-three minutes, he turned beetroot red. When I asked him about his favourite position, he turned crimson. Physical examination once again confirmed that our conversation had aroused him and my patient had no problem in that department.

My wife had a furrowed brow when she came out of her room. Something was bugging her but, true to her nature, she wasn't going to speak about it till she was a little more sure. She decided to get both of them together in one room again to quiz them about the sexual positions they preferred. Lambu was even more tongue-tied, given my wife's presence, and Bebe remained her silent self. However, my wife isn't the sort to give up easily. She wrote a note to our compounder, called Chotu in and, within half an hour, she had what she wanted. Lambu had demonstrated his preferred and only way of having sex using the dolls we use to demonstrate correct techniques with when my wife understood. She leaned forward and whispered to me, 'That was why the hymen was still intact!' And then, I knew too.

■

Lambu and Bebe gave birth to a baby girl almost exactly nine months to the day after we left their house. Tauji, in a bid to capture women's votes, praised the arrival of Goddess Lakshmi in his house (Chotu and Badi had two boys). He masked his disappointment at not getting another male heir well. About a year later, Bebe gave birth to a boy as well. And then, a year later, another boy. After that they called my wife so that she could explain some contraceptive techniques to her. They still can't pronounce her name right, though.

■

Tauji had been very curious about what his son and daughter-in-law had been doing wrong but we cited doctor-patient confidentiality and kept Lambu's secret, saving him from being the butt of many more jokes.

Tauji was effusive in his thanks. When the first child was born, he gifted us a four-bedroom apartment in a residential complex nearby. We set up our second clinic there, calling it The Tao Clinic. When our friends quiz us about it, we say that we have named it after a popular nightclub in New York. As part of the family's expansion plans, Lambu opened a pub in London. He offered us a stake in it which we gladly took up. In acknowledgement of our contribution to his successes, Lambu named the pub 'The Wrong Hole'. He tells me that it draws quite a good crowd.

■

A Tribute to Breasts (in Free Verse)

'What is it about these,
These two little hillocks, these mounds,
That fascinate you so?
I mean, just look at them!'
She said, cupping them, and fluidly changing their
    alluring shape.
She rolled her eyes, then,
When she saw mine
Gazing intently at her brilliant boobies,
Screamed, 'They are merely breasts!'

I, who am so ready with words,
Struggled to explain
What the fuss was about and
Decided to take the analytical approach,
De-emotionalize the issue.
(It wasn't easy to

Speak on behalf of all man-kind!)
'We, all of us…' I hesitated.
'Like stuff that we can evaluate,
using multiple criteria…'
I paused as a look of
Incredulity spread over her beautiful face.
'We guys, when we are just hanging out,
Can discuss breasts in so many ways.
Size: always a good place to start.
Shape: how curvy, how round are they?
Round or slim, full or like tiny spouts
Firmness: very important to us.
Direction: do both look ahead with steadfast gaze,
    or do they point in different directions?'

'But, surely,' she interrupted,
Dismissing my protestations
With an airy wave,
'Isn't it's just plain rude,
What you men do most of the days?
When speaking to someone,
Aren't you supposed to look them in the eye?
Last I checked, my eyes are here,'
She gestured towards her face,
'And definitely not here!'
She rubbed her perky nipples with forefinger and thumb.

It was my turn now
To ignore what she'd said.

I was now warming up,
Getting into the flow,
Summarizing effortlessly,
The countless discussions had over many a beer.
I knew I was getting through as
Her eyes widened.
She had obviously never thought of
Breasts having so many different dimensions
'How they fit into our hands is critical, too,' I said.
'Some perfectly fill a cupped palm,
Others spill out everywhere.
Squishiness is a nice feeling to get,
But so is springy firmness.'

It was she who was thoughtful now,
Pondering over what she'd just heard.

I took in a sharp, deep breath
And carried on,
'Which brings me to The Nipple,
The crowning glory.
The size, shape and colour of the areola,
Sets the tone for everything else.
The contrast between
The dusky areola and the duskier nipple,
Has afforded many an hour of debate pleasantly spent,
Nipples can be cute and button-shaped,
Or big circles which fill the mouth.
And even as The Nipples provide character,

They stir, and move,
And respond to the finger's touch.

She looked down at her hillocks with new respect,
She clearly saw much more now
Than she ever did before.
She said, softly, that she had only spoken
About men in general,
Not about me in particular.
She had never doubted my ability
To keep my gaze confined to the respectable areas
And never to stray.

'Men love that breasts look so different
From diverse angles.
From the side, like the about-to-rise sun,
Hidden partially but its magnificence about to reveal.
The cleavage, when viewed from above,
The furrow, when seen from below.
(If you are on top.)
The same breasts can take on such
Varied hues
Depending just on the view.'

'And last but in no way the least...'
I said, pressing on.
'It is the only other part of your wondrous body,
Which erects and,
Indicates that you are interested,

That I may get lucky tonight.'

She walked up,
Threw her arms around me,
And squashed the the twin subjects of our discussion
    against my chest.
Then, placing my arms around her,
She quietly asked
If I really could read all the signs
As well as I had just described.
And glancing saucily,
She undid, with slow, slow movements,
The top two buttons of her top.

As I sprang forward to help conclude,
What was proving to be a fruitful interlude,
I thanked my stars for my gifts of eloquence,
For the years I had spent debating,
And, of course, for the one thing I recommend,
More than anything else, to those
Desirous of following my fun-filled footsteps.
Reading books, lots of books,
Just like this, just like this.

■

Acknowledgements

A book, like a movie, is never an individual effort. Mine, especially, involved a lot of people.

My loving parents, Subhash and Rita Nagpal; I owe you everything for bringing me up the way you did, your love, the exposure and values you imparted. (I fully realize what a double-edged statement that is!)

My superlative kids, Anvam and Anvika. You bring zest to my life and a spring to my step. I feel younger and happier because of you.

The Book, Early Days

For valued encouragement, laughter in the right places and gentle, constructive criticism:
- Ritu Nagpal,
- Anu Menon,
- Neema Kapoor and
- Sandipan Deb.

Finding a Publisher

Sarita Mandana, world-famous author of *Tiger Hills* who—even though we hadn't been in touch after college—graciously agreed to help and put me in touch with Rupa Publications India.

Rashmi Agrawal Bansal, world-famous author of several books, friend and MBA batch mate who—even though the the subject matter wasn't really to her taste—guided me through the process of publication.

My Invaluable Support Group

My nani, Bimla Soni, my only surviving grandparent, a key part of my growing up, my big fan and also an important link to a different era, traditions and values.

My school gang, the bedrock of my existence in lots of ways:

- Amitabh and Neema Kapoor;
- Prashant and Rita Mishra;
- Sanjay and Sabrina Soni;
- Colonel Deepak Kapoor (We're proud of what you do for our country, buddy!) and Reena Kapoor;
- Sameer Sawhney, tragically taken away from us but who lives with us in memory, remembered in many conversations;
- A special shout out to Arun Kumar, Rahul Joneja and Avnish Madan;
- Sukanya Dutta Roy, for invaluable hand-holding, help, laughter, pep talks and drinks;
- Supriya Devnani Nagpal, for long-distance advice and giggles;
- Nitish and Neeti Kapoor, for a million favours, suggestions and support;

- Raghuvesh and Urvashi Sarup, for lots of excitement, energy, ideas and a touch of madness;
- Rohit and Alpana Chatterjee, for your amazing company, encouragement and a permanent pit-stop in Mumbai;
- Aditya and Seema Sehgal, for unflinching help whenever needed, all the way from China;
- Ravi and Pallavi Saxena for great, stimulating and encouraging company;
- Namrata Sharma for fantastic support, helping with lots of local Pune stuff, and tapping all her contacts to help;
- Tinu and Manu Randhawa, still miss you and your warmth as neighbours;
- Sandeep and Shefali Lakhina, for being fantastic hosts and for extending lots of help;
- Ravish Kumar, for sage advice and for help on many occasions;
- Anu Soni, a very special person, who has always encouraged me;
- My buas, for helping bring me up and for ensuring that I always had a huge extended family and lots of first cousins;
- Arun Soni, Aditi and Aman, you've always made me feel special;
- My neighbours, for tolerating my eccentricities and
- My very vibrant, eclectic group on Facebook and on Twitter.

Team Rupa

- Ravi Singh, for instilling belief in me and for believing in my work;
- Anurag Basnet, the editor I had always hoped for;
- Kapish Mehra, for quiet but firm support; and
- The rest of the team whom I am gradually getting to know better.

Team Eighteen Plus

- Nikhilesh and Nivedita Singh (Building Bridges Communication), for PR;
- Shakun Sethi, for guidance with social media;
- Vishal Bakaya, for execution in the social media space;
- Asit Gupta, for help with the marketing strategy;
- Malvika Mehra and Sandipan Deb, for finally delivering a great tagline;
- Enthrall Tech, especially Samir, Aditi, Asma, Nilesh and Sarika;
- Manish Jain, photographer;
- Swapn Gupta, photographer's assistant; and
- Anannya Giri, the cover model.

Taj Land's End, my home away from home in Mumbai.
Taj Vivanta, Gurgaon, my new base when in the city.

All my friends who helped promote the book including,
- Pratap Bose and his team, for their wonderful ideas and unbelievable help;
- Prashant Panday (Radio Mirchi) for his warmth and media support;
- Tarun Katial and the BigFM team;
- Neeraj Roy, who assured me of support from day one; and

The VH1 team and many more for help in so many ways.

www.ingramcontent.com/pod-product-compliance
Lightning Source LLC
Chambersburg PA
CBHW030330020726
47493CB00004B/1227